Discovery at Flint Springs

Discovery at Flint Springs

John R. Erickson

VIKING

VIKING
Published by Penguin Group
Penguin Young Readers Group, 345 Hudson Street, New York, New York 10014, U.S.A.
Penguin Group (Canada), 10 Alcorn Avenue, Toronto, Ontario, Canada M4V 3B2
(a division of Pearson Penguin Canada Inc.)
Penguin Books Ltd, 80 Strand, London WC2R 0RL, England
Penguin Ireland, 25 St Stephen's Green, Dublin 2, Ireland (a division of Penguin Books Ltd)
Penguin Group (Australia), 250 Camberwell Road, Camberwell, Victoria 3124, Australia
(a division of Pearson Australia Group Pty Ltd)
Penguin Books India Pvt Ltd, 11 Community Centre, Panchsheel Park, New Delhi - 110 017, India
Penguin Group (NZ), Cnr Airborne and Rosedale Roads, Albany, Auckland, New Zealand
(a division of Pearson New Zealand Ltd)
Penguin Books (South Africa) (Pty) Ltd, 24 Sturdee Avenue, Rosebank,
Johannesburg 2196, South Africa

Penguin Books Ltd, Registered Offices: 80 Strand, London WC2R 0RL, England

Published in 2004 by Viking, a division of Penguin Young Readers Group

1 3 5 7 9 10 8 6 4 2

LIBRARY OF CONGRESS CATALOGING-IN-PUBLICATION DATA
Erickson, John R., date-
Discovery at Flint Springs / John R. Erickson.
p. cm.
Summary: When Dr. Montrose visits their Texas ranch in the summer of 1927,
fourteen-year-old Riley and his twelve-year-old brother Coy are
drawn into an archeological adventure.
ISBN 0-670-05946-3 (hardcover)
[1. Brothers—Fiction. 2. Archaeology—Fiction. 3. Excavations
(Archaeology)—Fiction. 4. Texas—History—1865-1950—Fiction.] I. Title.
PZ7.E72556Di 2004
[Fic]—dc22
2004000495

Printed in U.S.A.

Set in Janson
Designed by Kelley McIntyre

To four heroes of Texas Panhandle archeology:
Douglas Boyd, Brett Cruse, Doug Wilkens,
and Danny Witt.

Chapter 1

I had known about Flint Springs most of my life. I could remember going there with my father when I was only three or four years old. It was a little flat-topped ridge on the west side of a spring that ran water year-round, and the edges of the ridge were littered with chips of flint and small rocks that appeared to have been burned.

"Indians lived here a long time ago," he said, "and this is all they left behind."

"When you were a boy?"

"No, before that, even before Grampy Dawson was a boy. They hunted with bows and arrows and lived in tepees."

"Tepees?"

"Shelters made of sticks and buffalo hide."

Sometimes we found an arrowhead lying among the scraps of flint, delicate triangles of stone that bore the marks of ancient craftsmen. Daddy let me have them, and I kept them in a corner of my clothes drawer, between my underpants my socks. I kept them for several years, then they disappeared. Maybe I traded them to kids at school or maybe they were victims of one of Mother's cleaning purges. For a while I considered them treasures, then they became tiresome little rocks in my drawer.

I didn't give much thought to the people who had lived at Flint Springs until the summer of 1927, nine months after my father had been killed in a horse accident. I was fourteen years old, and my little brother Coy was twelve. That was the summer I learned a new word: *archeology*.

On our ranch in the Texas Panhandle, the second half of July proved to be slow and tedious. It was hot, of course, but worse than hot. The wind, which was so much a part of our lives most of the time, stopped blowing, and an eerie silence fell across our valley. Grampy Dawson called this time the "dog days of summer."

Coy and I had spent the morning helping Grampy Dawson move some cattle up into Picket Canyon. When the wind quit blowing, our windmills didn't pump water. If the water level in the stock tanks got too low, we had to saddle our horses and move the cattle up into the canyons, where they could always find water at the springs.

That's what we had done, starting the work at 4:30 in the morning and getting the cattle relocated before the afternoon heat set in. After lunch, Grampy Dawson cranked up his old truck and drove into Canadian to check the mail. Spud Morris, our hired hand, went down to the barn to salvage parts off an old windmill motor. Mother had things to do inside the house. That left me and Coy alone on the porch.

There wasn't much for us to do but sit around in the shade, listening to the buzz of the yellow jacket wasps. It was kind of a boring day. Even our dog, Turk, seemed short on ambition. He found a shady spot beside the house, scratched up some damp dirt, and flopped down for a long nap.

Coy tried to make conversation. "Riley, what do you want to do when you grow up?"

"I'm already grown up. Don't forget that I have two black whiskers on my chin."

My little brother hated to be reminded that his little chin was as smooth as a baby's behind, while mine had sprouted two huge, glorious black hairs. "Riley, I'm trying to hold a serious conversation. Out of all the things in this world, what would you like to do?"

"It's too hot to think. You tell me what you want to be. I'm sure that's what you had in mind anyway."

Coy fixed his gaze on the heat waves that danced on the horizon. "I'm going to be a famous lion tamer. I'll travel to darkest Africa and trap the lions, then bring them back to America on a big ship. Along the way, we'll have many adventures with typhoons and pirates, but we'll finally make it to . . . some seaport on the West Coast."

"Salt Lake City?"

"No. Salt Lake City is in Utah, and it's not a seaport."

"School's out, Coy; we don't have to give right answers to everything."

He gave me a stubborn look. "Salt Lake City is in the middle of a desert, and it's not a seaport. It doesn't matter whether we're in school or not. Facts are facts and geography doesn't change."

"All right, suppose that someone built a canal from the ocean to Salt Lake City. Then your ship could follow the canal to Salt Lake City."

"Well, that would be silly. Why would anyone want to build a canal into a desert?"

"Because there aren't any mosquitoes in the desert. If you'd read your history, you'd know that when we built the Panama Canal, the mosquitoes were so bad, the workers caught yellow fever and died like flies. It was the wrong place to put a canal."

Coy shook his head and looked away. "Riley, that is the dumbest thing I ever heard."

"No, it's very sensible. Mosquitoes are a big problem. Why do you think they put the Suez Canal where they did? It's in the middle of a desert."

"Riley, they put the Suez Canal where they did because it connected the Red Sea with the Mediterranean Sea. They couldn't have put it anywhere else. It had nothing to do with mosquitoes."

"Well, that's your opinion, but let me point out that during the building of the Suez Canal, the French didn't lose a single worker to yellow fever."

"It was the British, Riley. The British built the Suez Canal."

"Okay, the British. Did they lose thousands of men to yellow fever? No. Why? No mosquitoes."

I enjoyed arguing with Coy. With very little effort I could steer him off the subject, and that always got him in an uproar. He glared at me through his oversized glasses and raised his voice. "Riley, I don't care about mosquitoes or canals. And I don't know how you always manage to—"

Just then Mother came to the door. Apparently we had disturbed her peace. "Boys, what's going on out here?"

Coy aimed a finger at me. "It's him. I was trying to make friendly conversation, trying to tell him that I wanted to be a lion tamer, and he . . . he pulled me into an argument about mosquitoes!"

Mother's gaze swung around to me. "Riley, are you teasing your brother?"

"No, we were discussing history and geography . . . biology, important things, and he just . . . I don't know, Mother, sometimes he seems so immature."

Coy's eyes rolled up inside his head. "Riley, you are

the biggest liar! Mother, I don't know how he does it, but I'll start off talking about a normal subject, and somehow he lures me into arguments that are just crazy. And he knows it too."

I raised my palms to express my innocence. "I don't know what he's talking about."

Mother pondered the case. "Boys, I think you have too much idle time, and I'm not going to listen to you snarl at each other all afternoon. Follow me." We followed her around to the north side of the house. With the toe of her shoe, she drew an X in the dirt. "Riley, I want you to dig me a hole on this spot, exactly twenty-five inches square and thirty-six inches deep."

"A hole for what?"

"We need to ventilate the ground."

Ventilate the ground? This had to be one of Grampy Dawson's "cures for an idle mind": dig a hole, fill it up, and dig another hole.

She moved ten steps to the east and drew another X. "Coy, you will dig a hole here, the same size and depth."

We were stunned. I said, "Mother, it's hot. It's roasting out here. This is cruel and unreasonable punishment."

She smiled. "I'll bring you a ruler." She went into the house and returned with a yardstick. She pointed to two shovels leaning against the house. "Don't disturb me until you're finished. If your hole isn't the right size, you'll dig another one."

It had begun to appear that she wasn't kidding. I tried

another approach. "Mother, last year a man from Canadian got heatstroke. It was in July, a day just like this."

"Really?"

"Yes ma'am, and I think he died."

"Mercy. Well, try not to get heatstroke." She went back into the house, leaving me and my little brother alone in the stifling heat.

Coy's face had twisted itself into a mask of anger. "Now look what you've done. I swear, I'll never speak to you again!"

We measured off our squares and started digging. The summer heat had baked the ground so that it was only slightly softer than granite. We hacked and chipped. Sweat rolled off my forehead and tickled a path down my spine. At the three-inch depth, I stopped and leaned on my shovel.

"You know, Coy, if you weren't such a baby, we could have worked things out ourselves." No response. "There was no need to get Mother involved in this. Coy, are you listening?"

He kept on digging. "I'm listening but I'm not talking to you."

"If we don't talk, this is going to be a long afternoon."

"I don't care. Talking to you is hopeless. You twist things into knots and get me in trouble."

"It's sad when brothers can't talk." No answer. "I guess that being a part of this family doesn't mean much to you." That didn't draw him out either. "Okay, it was all my fault. I was bored and I pulled you into a silly argument."

He looked at me. "You're just saying that."

"No, I'm being sincere. I was a rat, and I'm sorry."

"Well"—he wiped his forehead—"all right, if you're serious."

"I am. Brothers shouldn't do this to each other. Family is just too important."

"Well . . . okay, but you've got to promise to stop getting me in trouble."

"Done. Now, why don't you go to the well house and get us a bucket of water?"

Coy brightened. "That's a great idea. She didn't say we couldn't stop for a drink."

He dropped his shovel and trotted off toward the well house. As soon as he rounded the corner of the house, I slipped over to his hole and started filling it with dirt.

Chapter 2

I knew it was an ornery prank, but the digging project was making me desperate for some kind of relief. Suddenly I heard a voice behind me.

"Riley, clean out Coy's hole. *Immediately.*"

The voice startled me. I jumped and whirled around. Mother's face was framed in the kitchen window. She had seen it all.

"Yes ma'am."

"And when your grandfather gets back from town, he'll speak to you about being disobedient to your mother and mean to your brother."

"Yes ma'am."

Her face disappeared inside the house. Now I knew the awful truth: not only had we been sentenced to a chain gang, but there were spies watching our every move. I had just about removed the last of the dirt from Coy's hole when he returned with the pail of water.

He saw me working in his hole. "What are you doing?"

I stopped, wiped the sweat out of my eyes, and leaned on the shovel. "Well, you went for the water, so I thought the least I could do was, you know, help you out a little bit with the digging."

"Really?"

"We're brothers, Coy, and the older ones should help the younger ones."

"Gee, I don't know what to say. Thanks."

We drank our fill, threw water on our faces, dampened our shirts, and returned to the slavery that had been imposed upon us by a cruel mother. Thirty minutes later, I was fed up with digging.

"Coy, I have an idea."

He gave me a wary look. "That usually means trouble for me."

"Not this time. This will work."

Coy was full of doubts, and it took me a while to win him over. I ran into the house and found Mother sewing a patch on a pair of Grampy's jeans.

"Mother, come quick. Something's wrong with Coy. I think the heat has gotten him."

Mother let out a gasp and followed me out the door. We ran around the side of the house. There lay poor Coy, stretched out on the ground, moaning and twitching.

Mother studied the scene for a moment, then seized the bucket and threw water in Coy's face. He wasn't expecting that. His eyes popped open and he gurgled for air. Mother bobbed her head up and down, her suspicions confirmed. "Get up off that ground, Coy McDaniels, before I skin you alive."

"Yes ma'am," he sputtered, groping for his shovel.

Then she turned to me, her lips compressed into a tight line. "And you, Mr. Agitator, will dig your hole all the way to China. You're not to stop digging until you can show me *a pair of chopsticks.*"

She marched back into the house. In the silence, I heard my little brother say, "You think you're so smart. I told you it wouldn't work."

"Coy, it would have worked if you'd done a better job of acting. People with sunstroke don't twitch and quiver like that."

Coy muttered something under his breath but said no more. We returned to our circles of silence and dug for another half hour. It was then that I heard an odd hum in the distance. It was a motor of some kind. I shaded my eyes and looked off to the southwest.

"Coy, look. It's an airplane."

"Forget it, Riley. I'm not as gullible as you think."

"Coy, it's an airplane."

"Airplanes never fly over us."

He was right about that. Our ranch wasn't close to any major airport, and we seldom saw flying machines. When we did, it was something special.

The hum grew louder, and at last Coy had to admit

that he heard it too. He straightened up and squinted into the distance. "Well, I'll be. It is an airplane."

We watched. The hum grew louder, and the airplane seemed to be coming toward our house. I said, "I'm going to tell Mother. She'll want to see this."

I hurried into the house. When the screen door slammed behind me, Mother flinched and beamed me a hostile look. "Riley, I've just about had enough of your—"

"Mother, come look. There's an airplane flying this way."

I don't think she believed me at first, but then she heard the drone of the engine. We trooped outside and joined Coy in front of the house.

He said, "Riley, look, it's not a biplane. It only has one wing."

Indeed, it had only a single wing. That was a fairly new development in aircraft design, one that had appeared after the end of the Great War in Europe. Back in May, a man named Charles Lindbergh had flown a single-wing aircraft from Westbury, New York, all the way across the Atlantic Ocean to Paris, France. His flight had made front-page headlines all over the world. We had heard about it from our friend Aaron Kaplan, while we were visiting in Sparrow, Texas; otherwise we might not have known about it for months.

Out where we lived, news traveled slowly.

Mother seemed excited about seeing the airplane and, for the moment at least, she had forgotten about the digging. Shielding her eyes with both hands, she said, "You know, boys, I think it's going to fly right over the house. And it's . . . oh my stars, it's coming down! It's going to crash into the house! Run!"

This seemed incredible: the first airplane we had seen in months, and as Mother had said, it had gone into a dive and was heading straight for our house. We ran for cover beneath a grove of chinaberry trees and watched. Spud Morris came out of the barn to see what was going on. He was half deaf, but even he had heard the roar of the engine. His mouth hung open, and he stared at the looming disaster.

Mother clutched us in a tight grip. We watched and waited for our house to go up in a ball of orange gasoline flames. The plane came closer and closer. It was headed straight for the house. Then, at the last second, the nose came up, and the plane went screaming past, climbing and banking to the left.

Mother caught her breath. "Well, I never . . . the man must be drunk!"

But I had noticed something. As the plane skimmed over the roof of the house, the pilot had tossed something out the window. I kept my eyes on the spot where it had landed and ran to it. It was an ordinary caliche rock, but attached to it was a piece of paper tied with twine.

It appeared to be some kind of note.

 **Chapter 3**

By the time I had gotten the note out of the twine, Mother and Coy had joined me. I glanced at the note and laughed. "Holy cow, listen to this: 'I'm going to land on your road. Please prepare cool drinks for two, and cookies would be nice. Aaron.'"

We were all too astonished to speak. The only Aaron we knew was Aaron Kaplan, our friend from Sparrow.

Mother said, "Heavenly days! What is he doing in an airplane?"

None of us had the answer to that, but we didn't have long to wait. The pilot set the plane down on our dirt road, spun it around, and taxied toward the house.

Turk, our loyal dog, had been jolted out of his afternoon nap and had gone into a frenzy of defensive barking, but once he saw the plane coming his way, old Turk went into full retreat and vanished under the house.

The plane stopped beside the yard gate, and the pilot shut off the engine. The propeller chopped the air a few more times and died. The door, which was located on the left side of the plane, near the middle, popped open, and out stepped Aaron Kaplan, with a mischievous grin and a twinkle in his dark eyes. Behind him came an older man with a trimmed gray beard, dressed in khaki clothes and a wide-brimmed straw hat. I didn't recognize him.

I had never seen Aaron in anything but a suit and tie, usually with a vest, but now he wore jeans, a cotton work shirt, and a pair of high-top lace-up boots. If I hadn't known it was Aaron, I might have thought he was an explorer from England or somewhere back east.

Smiling, he brushed the dust off his pants and approached us. "You look surprised."

Mother offered her hand. "Aaron, I expect that kind of mischief from these boys, but honestly! What are you doing out here . . . and flying an airplane?"

Aaron was enjoying himself. "In time, in time." He shook hands with me and Coy, then motioned toward the stranger. "Sara McDaniels, Coy and Riley, I'd like for you to meet Dr. Francis Montrose of the Peabody Museum in Cambridge, Massachusetts."

Aaron gave the name *Peabody* the Boston pronunciation: not "PEA-body," as any Texan would have said it, but "Peabiddy."

We greeted the stranger, a man with deep blue-gray

eyes and a dignified bearing, then Coy and I bombarded Aaron with questions. He lifted a single finger in the air and brought it to his lips. "Patience. Do you suppose we could have a drink of water?"

We went inside and seated ourselves around the kitchen table. I noticed that Dr. Montrose took in every detail of our house, from the baseboards to the trim along the ceiling, as though he had never seen the inside of a Texas ranch house.

Mother served up big glasses of water for the men and brought out the last of a peach pie she had baked the day before. At last, when he had nearly drained his glass, Aaron was ready to address our questions.

Mother said, "I didn't know you were a pilot."

His shoulders rose and fell. "I never got around to mentioning it. Actually, I've been flying for several years but only recently acquired my own airplane."

Coy said, "Yeah, and what a plane! It's huge."

"It is, isn't it? It's quite a bit more than I need, but it was part of a bankruptcy auction in Cleveland, Ohio, and it sold for a fraction of its value. It's a bit gaudy, but I couldn't pass it up."

Mother said, "You were in Cleveland, Ohio?"

"Oh no. I have people who buy things for me. It's an early prototype of the Lockheed Vega. It was intended to be a cargo plane, along the lines of the Ford Trimotor, only smaller and faster. But I've equipped it with seats. It can carry six passengers at one hundred thirty-five miles per hour, and it has a range of five hundred miles. It has the very latest instrumentation, and it's top of the line. When I bought it, it had only two hundred hours on the engine. I'd be embarrassed to tell you how little I paid for it."

Aaron took the last sip of his water and gestured toward his friend. "Dr. Montrose is an archeologist and has come to Texas to do a survey of prehistoric sites along the Canadian River. We've spent the afternoon flying over the Alibates ruins south of Amarillo, and I thought we'd stop in for a visit. Frank thinks there might be some archeological sites on your ranch."

Mother's head wagged from side to side. "Aaron, you've never said one word to us about archeology."

He smiled. "I knew very little about archeology until Frank walked into my store three days ago. He needed help in getting permission to look at sites on private land, and since I'm the mayor, he came to me. He informed me that there are some important prehistoric sites near Sparrow."

Coy perked up. "Prehistoric? You mean dinosaurs?"

"Oh no. Dinosaurs are much older, but I'll let Dr. Montrose tell you about the sites, since he's one of the country's leading experts." Aaron looked at Mother. "Maybe I should ask if we're interrupting anything."

Mother couldn't suppress a chuckle. "Hardly. The boys had gotten bored and were bickering, so I put them to work digging holes behind the house."

Aaron's brows rose. "Digging? Hmmm. That might come in handy." He turned to Dr. Montrose. "Frank, why don't you tell them about the Panhandle Aspect sites?"

Dr. Montrose had brought a rolled-up map with him. He cleared the table and unfurled it. It was a map of the south-central United States and included the states of Texas, Oklahoma, and Kansas, as well as eastern New Mexico, southern Colorado, and southern Nebraska.

He cleared his throat and began. "We call this region the Southern Plains. When Coronado explored the region in 1540, he found groups of people who lived in permanent houses and cultivated corn and other crops. We know quite a bit about the Puebloans in New Mexico and the Caddos to the east, but these groups in the middle"—his finger drew a circle around the Texas and Oklahoma Panhandles—"are a bit of a mystery. Very little scientific work has been done here.

"Eight years ago, in 1919, Dr. Warren Moorehead of Andover Academy in Massachusetts did an exploration and survey of the Canadian River valley. What he found surprised everyone: more than a hundred sites that had rectangular stone foundations and evidence of heavy occupation. It appears that the people who built them came into the region sometime around 1200 and by the time Coronado passed through in 1540, they were gone. Moorehead gave this group of ruins the name Panhandle Aspect."

Dr. Montrose rolled up the map, took his seat, and continued. "As Aaron told you, there is a major concentration of these Panhandle Aspect sites along the tributaries of the Canadian River, within a fifty-mile radius of Sparrow. These sites are a national treasure, a storehouse of information that is absolutely unique and irreplaceable. Unfortunately, they're being destroyed at a rate that sickens the heart. Aaron, you tell them."

Aaron nodded and rose from his chair. He plunged his hands into his pockets and prowled the room as he talked. "When oil was discovered a year and a half ago, Hutchinson County was flooded with a migration of people. Almost overnight, Sparrow became a city of more than five thousand. Construction crews began leveling land for drilling rigs, roads were cut to the locations, and, as you might expect, no one in the oil field was giving much thought to the archeological sites they might be destroying in the process. That seems to be the story of progress. When we build one thing, we destroy another.

"But that's only the beginning. Last May, two months ago, we imposed the rule of law upon our unruly community. You"—he nodded toward Mother, me, and Coy—"were there and had a front-row seat, so you know the story very well. With the help of the Texas Rangers, our reform group ousted the gangsters who had been running things and we made it safe for commerce and law-abiding citizens. In one lightning coup, we seized the town and sent the rascals on their way.

"Most of the criminal element moved on to boom-towns in Oklahoma and West Texas, but others remained. I'm sorry to say that some of them have turned to looting these archeological sites, these 'national treasures,' as Frank described them."

Dr. Montrose nodded and returned to the discussion. "For decades, even centuries, there has been a lively trade in antiquities and treasures: Egyptian, Greek, Roman, Mesopotamian, Aztec, Mayan, Incan. This shabby business has pitted the forces of science against a determined group of traders who rip open tombs and ancient dwellings in search of artifacts and trinkets that they peddle to wealthy individuals who have nothing better to do than to amass collections."

The doctor's eyes crackled and he pounded his fist on the table. "These looters are the enemy. They're not only the enemy of archeologists, they're the enemy of the entire human community, because they're erasing our memory of the past. When they rip an artifact out of the ground, they destroy its context. It becomes a trinket that tells us nothing about when it was made or how it might have been used. Looters care nothing about knowledge, only the dollars they can make selling these trinkets. It's disgraceful!"

He was silent for a moment, then smiled at his own outburst. "Sorry; I get stirred up when I talk about this. Without context, we archeologists are blind. We have no information, just an object that can't tell us anything about itself."

Aaron turned to Mother. "Well, that's probably more than you wanted to know about archeology."

"Not at all. I'm fascinated, and I'm sure the boys are too."

Coy and I nodded. Not only was I interested in this lesson on Panhandle archeology, but I was more than vaguely aware that we had been released from the bondage of digging holes in the backyard.

Aaron continued. "Frank and I don't expect to make archeologists out of you in one session, but all of this does have a point. Nobody knows what archeological sites might be on your ranch, or on any of these isolated ranches in the northeastern Panhandle. But this much we know, Sara. As long as there's a market for antiquities, clever men will supply the demand. We're trying to put a stop to some of the plundering around Sparrow, and if we do, the diggers will be scouting for a new source."

"Here?"

"Yes. If they haven't already tried to rob your sites, it may be just a matter of time until they get to them."

Mother thought for a moment. "Well, what can we do?"

"That's why we're here. The first thing we need to do is locate the sites. Frank is pretty good at spotting them from the air. Why don't we load up in the Vega and take a look?"

Coy and I could hardly conceal our excitement. Neither of us had ever ridden in an airplane before.

Mother stared at Aaron and barked a funny little laugh. "Fly in an aircraft? No thank you, and I'd rather the boys didn't either."

Chapter 4

Our hopes were dashed. Coy and I traded looks, then went to work on Mother. Coy took the lead. "Mother, this is the chance of a lifetime! Please? Pleeeeease?"

Mother folded her arms across her chest and shook her head. It was time for me to swing into action. "Mother, you've always wanted us to expand our horizons and learn about the world beyond the ranch. Airplanes are part of the modern world, and I'm sure you'll agree that this would be a great opportunity for us to learn more about them. It would be very educational. I'm sure you agree."

"I don't agree."

"Mother! All right, if you don't want to fly, at least let Coy and me go up."

Her chin rose to a stubborn angle. "Riley, do you

know how many pilots for the post office have died in crashes since 1918?"

"Well . . . no."

"Thirty-one. The post office discontinued its airmail service in May."

"How did you know that?"

"I read it in the newspaper the last time we went to the library. Flying is unnatural for human beings. If God had wanted us to fly, he would have made us with wings."

I didn't know how to argue with that. I looked to Aaron for help. He was standing behind Mother's chair and made a gesture with his hand that told me to back off. He said, "Why don't we go out to the Vega and take a look?"

Mother hesitated, then rose from her chair. "I'll look, but I'm not getting in that thing."

Aaron slipped his arm through Mother's and they walked outside. Coy and I followed, and Dr. Montrose came along behind us. On the way to the airplane, Aaron spoke to Mother in a quiet voice.

"Flying is probably more natural to humans than you think. After all, the same God who made birds gave us the ability to dream and invent."

"Aaron, that thing is huge. It must weigh a ton."

"It weighs four thousand pounds, empty."

"You see? It weighs *two tons*, and anything that weighs two tons has no business leaving the ground. You'll never convince me that it's natural for people to be flying around in those contraptions."

They had reached the Vega by this time. Aaron put his hand on the propeller and continued talking in that same soothing tone of voice. "Actually, the weight of an aircraft is irrelevant. What matters is thrust and lift. It's all a matter of simple physics. If you can generate enough thrust through the engine and propeller, and enough lift on the wings, there's no limit to the size or weight of the aircraft. In theory, we could build airplanes as big as your house."

He told her about the engine, the aerodynamic shape of the propeller blade, and the shape of the wings, which caused air to flow over the top, creating lift. "The early inventors—the Wrights, Curtiss, and others—were imitating the shape of birds' wings. Every part of a bird, from its beak to its feathers, is a masterpiece of aerodynamic engineering. We've merely copied the blueprint of nature."

Mother was weakening but not ready to give up. She looked him straight in the eyes. "Aaron, let me speak frankly. My boys are all I have. I'm not ready to send them up in a flying contraption with a man who—"

Aaron finished the sentence for her. "A man who just recently learned to fly?"

"Yes. I don't mean to be rude, but that bothers me."

Aaron brushed a yellow jacket wasp off her shoulder. "Would it surprise you to know that I was flying for the army during the war?"

For a moment she couldn't speak. "Yes, it certainly *would* surprise me. Were you?"

He smiled. "I flew forty-seven scouting missions in

three different aircraft. I'm a pretty good pilot."

Dr. Montrose had been listening, and he nodded. "I can vouch for that. He's an excellent pilot."

Mother said, "Aaron, you're impossible! You let me blunder along and make a fool of myself. Why didn't you tell me this before?"

"We've never had the time, and I didn't want to bore you."

She looked away and muttered something under her breath. "All right, take the boys. If I don't let them go, they'll think I'm a witch."

Aaron was silent for a moment, rocking up and down on his toes. "I think you'd enjoy flying. It's an exhilarating experience. The air is smooth today, so it would be a nice flight."

"Aaron, don't push. No."

But Aaron Kaplan wasn't one to give up easily. It took him another ten minutes of coaxing, but he finally managed to get her inside the plane and strapped down in one of the four seats that ran the length of the interior. She was pale and grim-lipped, but she was there, sitting behind me and Coy. Her last words on the subject were, "Well, if my boys go down in a crash, I might as well go with them."

Aaron and Dr. Montrose took the pilot and copilot seats. Aaron started the engine, warmed it up, and checked out his instruments. Then we taxied south down the dirt road for a mile, turned around, and taxied back to the house. I thought something might have gone wrong, but Aaron called out, "Checking for cows on the runway."

That's something I wouldn't have thought of. Meeting a cow in the middle of takeoff wouldn't be good.

In front of the house, Aaron swung the Vega around into the south wind, set his flaps, and hit full throttle. Suddenly, we felt the power of the machine. The plane roared away in a cloud of dust, pressing us back into our seats. Objects flew past in a blur. All I could say was, "Wow!"

Behind me, I heard Mother gasp, "Good Lord!"

And then we were above the ground, floating and climbing. Down below, our cows in the mesa pasture had become the size of toys. Aaron banked to the left, adjusted the throttle, and then leveled off. We flew over the rim of Picket Canyon and headed toward the east pasture.

Up front, Dr. Montrose had opened up a map of the Canadian River valley and was comparing what he saw on the map with the view down below. Over the roar of the engine, I could hear some of his conversation with Aaron.

"Let's look at the mouth of that canyon. Those big cottonwood trees tell us there's water close to the surface, probably a running spring. Always go to the cottonwoods. Nine out of ten times, you'll find a campsite above the spring. Early man was drawn to wood and water."

He made a note on his map. We flew over the rest of the pasture, and the professor noted several other sites that he thought looked promising. When we flew up

Point Creek Canyon, I yelled out, "That's where we found the still, Aaron. That's Moonshine Springs."

He nodded, remembering that back in May, a gang of crooks had moved onto our ranch and had set up an illegal moonshining business at the spring. He banked the plane to the left, and headed for the west side of the ranch.

Up front, Dr. Montrose said, "I'm surprised there's no sign of stone houses in that valley. Maybe the terrain was too rough for farming. Plains Village people were looking for farmland. When you're scouting for Plains Village occupation, you look for the richest soils, places where they could grow corn."

Aaron nodded and guided the plane over Hodges Mesa. There, we got a broad view of the west pasture. Dr. Montrose said, "Ah, this looks more like farm country. See how the valley widens out? Unless I'm mistaken, we'll see the outlines of houses in this valley, probably on top of those ridge toes."

We flew across the pasture from east to west, then crossed it from north to south, from the deep canyon we called Big Rocks down to the south fence line. The doctor made some notes on his map, but I noticed that he was scowling.

"I don't understand. If this valley were up the river around Sparrow, we'd see dozens of stone outlines, clear evidence of Plains Village occupation. I don't see any of it here." He pointed to a line of trees down below. "Let's take a look at that. It's another spring."

He was pointing to Flint Springs.

Aaron banked the plane and went down for a closer look. Dr. Montrose made some notes on the map, then said, "It's a perfect habitation site, but I see no structures. Where are the houses? Aaron, I'd like to walk over that site, if we have time."

Ten minutes later, we were on the ground, parked in front of the house. Aaron climbed out of his seat and opened the door for us. Coy and I jumped out of the plane, while Aaron took Mother's hand and helped her down. We were all curious to hear what she would say. During the flight, she hadn't made a sound.

Aaron said, "Well, what did you think of your first voyage in a flying machine?"

She gave him a lopsided grin. "The first five minutes were terrifying. After that, I began to enjoy it. Thank you for being pushy and overbearing and making me go."

I could see that Aaron was pleased, and also amused at the way she had said it, calling him "pushy and overbearing." He chuckled to himself, then looked at his pocket watch. "Frank wants to walk across that last site we looked at. I was wondering if your father might drive us over there in his truck." Aaron frowned and glanced around. "Come to think of it, where is Abner?"

Before Mother could tell him that Grampy had gone to town for the mail, we heard his old Model T truck coming our way, chugging and making an orchestra of squeaks and rattling sounds. He parked the truck beside the barn and came walking toward us, his eyes on the plane and a little smirk tugging at the left side of his mouth.

He offered Aaron his hand. "Hello, son, good to see you again. Does that thing belong to you?"

"Yes, it's new. What do you think?"

Grampy studied the plane. "Looks pretty nice. Did you build it yourself?"

There was a moment of shocked silence, then Aaron burst out laughing. Ordinarily, he was a fairly serious fellow, but around Abner Dawson, it was hard to be serious for very long. Aaron introduced Grampy to Dr. Montrose and explained the purpose of their visit.

"We wondered if you might drive us over to the place you call Flint Springs," Aaron said. "We could walk, but I'm afraid we'd run out of daylight."

Grampy said he'd be glad to drive us to the spring.

There was never any question that Coy and I would go along, but I was a little surprised that Mother joined us. She rode in the cab with Grampy, while the rest of us loaded ourselves on the flatbed in the back, and off we went. The road to the west pasture climbed a fairly steep hill, which was actually the northern end of the mesa that divided the mesa pasture and the west pasture. There was very little barbed wire fence between the two pastures, as the steep sides of the mesa provided a natural barrier that kept cattle from crossing.

In times of rain or snow, that road to the west pasture

was impassable. In fair weather, it was merely steep and rough. At the base of the hill, Grampy pressed down the low-gear pedal and we crawled our way up to the crest. There the question became, did the old truck have enough brakes to slow our descent and keep us from wrecking at the bottom? We eased our way down the other side, with the brakes making squeaks and squeals that didn't inspire a lot of confidence.

I noticed that Dr. Montrose had a worried expression on his face all the way down the hill. It appeared that riding in Grampy's truck was giving him more of a scare than swooping over the ranch in Aaron's flying machine.

Chapter 5

Grampy kept driving toward Flint Springs, and when we got there we all climbed out of the truck. The site was located on a ridge toe that rose fifty or sixty feet above the spring. As we approached, Dr. Montrose pointed to the ground.

"This is the kind of surface debris that's always present around a habitation site: round quartzite cobbles, burned rock, cracked rock, flint chips, and pieces of bone." He pointed to the lip of the ridge toe. "You see there? The cultural debris is just gushing out of that toe. We call it midden debris. A midden was a trash dump. Prehistoric people produced a certain amount of garbage from cooking, eating, processing food, and building tools, and they usually tossed their trash over the edges of these ridge toes, or sometimes into pits. A midden deposit is an archeologist's treasure. A people's garbage can tell us a lot about who they were."

He bent down and picked up a piece of flint. He held it up to his eyes and turned it around, looking at all sides. "Here we go: our first diagnostic artifact. This is a beautiful specimen, symmetrical and well crafted by an expert flint-knapper." He handed the point to Aaron, who studied it and passed it around. "We call that a Scallorn point. This style is notched at the corners and has a barb on either side. It was most commonly used during the Woodland period, which means that it was made between one thousand and two thousand years ago."

Mother was surprised. "You mean people were living here that long ago? I had always thought of arrowheads being maybe two or three hundred years old."

"That's a common misconception, Mrs. McDaniels. Many times when novices find an arrowhead, they assume it belonged to one of the tribes that were here when the first European settlers arrived—the Comanches, Kiowas, and Southern Cheyennes, the people depicted in moving pictures and western novels. But those tribal Indians were latecomers to this region, arriving here from the north in the 1700s. You seldom find archeological material around their occupations."

"Why is that?" Mother asked.

"By the 1700s, the Plains Indians had acquired steel from French and Mexican traders and they were making their arrow points of steel instead of flint. Steel weathers and rusts away over time, and the points rarely ever survive. Also, the Plains tribes were horse nomads. They followed the bison herds and lived in tents made of bison hides."

"Tepees?"

"Exactly. When they moved, they took their tepees with them. They didn't build permanent structures, so they left nothing behind for meddlesome archeologists to find."

Coy had been listening to all of this. "You mean, all this stuff on the ground is a thousand years old?"

The doctor nodded. "At least. A spring site like this provided drinking water, firewood, freshwater mussels, and sometimes fish. It was an oasis in the desert and it could have layer upon layer of occupation. The oldest horizons could date back five or ten thousand years. One of the objectives of a controlled excavation is to expose the different levels of occupation as we go down, and to establish a date for each level. Remember context? When we find a tool or a piece of bone in the context of a soil profile, we can make a guess at the date."

"It sounds complicated," said Coy.

"Well, it's science, my boy, and yes, it's quite a bit more involved than picking up arrowheads off the ground. That Scallorn point gives us some clue as to the age of this site, but if we found it side by side with a shard of pottery and a piece of bison bone, it would tell us that the same people who made the Scallorn point also made ceramic pots and hunted bison. We could place all three objects in a date range of one to two thousand years ago."

Dr. Montrose glanced at the location of the sun and excused himself, saying that he wanted to make a rapid walk over the entire site while it was still light enough to see. As the rest of us strolled around looking for artifacts on the surface, the doctor made his survey, walking with his eyes to the ground and his hands clasped behind his back.

While we were waiting, Mother asked Grampy about his trip into Canadian. "Did we get any mail?"

"A picture-show calendar. There's another W. C. Fields movie coming to Canadian this month."

Mother wrinkled her nose at the mention of the famous Hollywood actor and said, "Ugh." She considered Fields a nasty old man and didn't like his movies.

Grampy said, "And I got a letter from Sleepy Joe Harper."

"Who's that?"

"He's a fiddle player down at Mineral Wells." Grampy gazed off into the distance. "He wondered if I could come down and play a few deals with him."

An awkward silence moved between Mother and Grampy. Grampy's fiddle playing was a touchy subject. In his younger days, Abner Dawson had built quite a name for himself as a musician, but to do it, he'd spent too much time away from his family. Both he and my mother had felt some regrets about that, and now that she was a widow raising two boys, Grampy had stopped playing dances and was staying with us on the ranch.

She said, "What will you tell him?"

"Well, sugar, I'll tell him I have other responsibilities."

Mother nodded and said no more about it.

Dr. Montrose rejoined us about twenty minutes later. His face was flushed from the hiking, and his eyes were sparkling. Aaron asked what he'd seen.

"This is a very interesting site," he said. "The amount of cultural debris here suggests a typical village occupation, but . . . " He tossed his hands into the air. "Where are the stone foundations? Where are the houses?"

I glanced around to see if anyone else would ask why those stone foundations were so important. Nobody asked, so I did.

Dr. Montrose said, "Riley, conventional theory says this site should be a copy of other Plains Village sites in the Panhandle—permanent houses with rectangular stone foundations that are easy to see. But this is something different: no rectangles of stone, just a few isolated rocks here and there, and very little pottery. It appears to be a Woodland site, hundreds of years older than the sites around Sparrow, and it could give us critical information about the people who occupied this valley one to two thousand years ago. Nobody has ever reported a site quite like this one."

He gestured toward the ridge. "And most important, this site is pristine. It's never been plundered or vandalized. We must make every effort to protect it until someone can do a controlled excavation." He turned to Mother. "Mrs. McDaniels, it appears that you are the custodian of an archeological treasure."

Mother blinked her eyes in surprise, then turned to me. "Gracious, is that something we want?"

"I think it's pretty exciting."

Her expression said she wasn't so sure about that.

By the time we made it back to the house, the sun had dropped behind Hodges Mesa and the valley had begun to melt into the purple shadows of evening. This seemed a matter of concern to Aaron, since the landing strip at Sparrow didn't have electric lights for night landings.

Mother said, "You're welcome to stay for supper and spend the night. Fly back tomorrow when it's safer."

"Sara, we don't want to impose on your hospitality." Mother's eyes narrowed in mock anger. Aaron made a gesture of surrender. "Well, we did throw our bedrolls into the back of the Vega, just in case."

"Good. I'll start supper. It won't be fancy, but you won't go hungry."

Aaron and Dr. Montrose hauled their bedrolls out of the baggage compartment at the rear of the plane. Grampy walked beside Aaron and said, "Son, I don't reckon you thought to bring your fiddle, did you?"

Aaron grinned. "As a matter of fact, Abner, I did."

We went into the house. Coy helped Mother throw together a meal of scrambled eggs, bacon, biscuits, and warmed-up pinto beans while I prepared the kerosene lamps for the coming night. Grampy and Aaron brought out their instruments and played until supper was on the table.

Aaron was actually a *violinist* rather than a fiddle player, and all his training had been in the area of classical music, but he made no secret that he admired Grampy's style of playing the old fiddle tunes and reels, songs that he played by ear and had learned from other fiddlers.

After supper, by the light of three kerosene lamps, Aaron learned "Cripple Creek" in the Abner Dawson style, and soon they were playing it together as double fiddles. Dr. Montrose sat in a corner, watching and tapping his foot until, around ten o'clock, he fell asleep in his chair.

Mother, Coy, and I enjoyed the show. We'd heard Grampy Dawson play many times, but it never got old or tiresome. Something magic came over him when he tucked that fiddle under his chin, tapped the toe of his boot on the floor, and tore into the strings with his bow.

Aaron might have been a better technician on the instrument, but he didn't have the passion or energy that Grampy put into it, and Aaron was the first to admit it. After playing along with Grampy on a few numbers, he placed his violin in his lap and listened with the rest of us.

Around eleven o'clock, Grampy yawned and put his fiddle back in the case. In the silence, Mother said, "Daddy, I think you should go down to Mineral Wells."

He sat up straight and stared at her. "What?"

"Go on and play that fiddle for other people. That's what you're supposed to do on this earth."

"What about you and the boys?"

"There isn't much to do around here in the summer except check the water and put out salt. Spud and the boys can handle it. I'm not trying to run you off, Daddy, but I don't want to hold you here. You came back when we really needed you, and I'm ready to share you a little bit."

Grampy smiled. "Thanks, honey, I'll give it some thought."

We all said good night and went to bed. Grampy went down to his usual place, the barn, and Aaron and the doctor rolled their beds out in the grass in front of the house. Mother tried to coax them inside, but they could see that our house wasn't big enough for guests. It was hardly even big enough for us: Mother's bedroom, the kitchen-dining room, a living room, and the screened porch. To give Mother some privacy, I slept on a bedroll on the porch, while Coy made his bed on the couch.

I drifted off to sleep thinking about archeology—and happy that Mother had forgotten all about punishing Coy and me for our transgressions.

Chapter 6

When I awoke the next morning, I heard Mother building a fire in the kitchen stove. It was six o'clock and nobody but Mother was stirring, so I rolled over to grab a little more sleep. Then I heard quiet footsteps enter the house. I cracked my eyes and saw that it was Aaron, fresh and ready for the day.

He tiptoed into the kitchen and pulled a chair over to the stove, where Mother was preparing breakfast. She handed him a cup of hot coffee. After a moment of silence, she said, "The boys and I are glad to see you again. Thank you for coming."

"It doesn't take much of an excuse."

"Your visits mean a lot to us."

"Thank you. This family has certainly warmed my life."

"I just wish it weren't so far. But now that you have the airplane, maybe you can come more often."

Aaron gazed up at the ceiling. "I hadn't thought of that." Mother gave him a sideward glance, and they seemed to share a smile. Then Aaron said, "I'm a little concerned about your father leaving. Are you sure you'll be all right out here?"

"We got along for six months before Daddy came back. It was all right until the moonshiners showed up." She clasped the handle of her big cast iron skillet in both hands and placed it on the stove. "The thing is, Aaron, I don't want to be a clinging vine. Daddy has this wonderful talent, and I want him to go out and share it with the world. He's no rancher; he never has been. He's a musician and a performer, and he needs to go where people can appreciate his gifts."

Aaron watched her as she placed strips of bacon into the skillet. "That's a noble thing to say."

"No, it's just recognizing the way things are. I'd like Daddy to come back as often as he can, but I don't want to hold him here."

Aaron took a sip of coffee. "I wish you had a telephone, so you could call me if you needed something."

"We'll never get a telephone out here. I've asked about it. The cost of the poles alone would be prohibitive."

"Maybe you don't need poles."

She glanced down at him. "What do you mean? The

phone company always runs the wires on poles."

Aaron smiled and drank his coffee.

After breakfast, Aaron and Dr. Montrose rolled up their bedding and loaded it into the plane. We all gathered in front of the house to say our good-byes. The doctor thanked Mother for her hospitality and said, "I have another week's survey work to do in the western part of the Panhandle, but before I go back to Massachusetts, I'd like to come back here and do some testing on that site. The more I think about it, the more it fascinates me."

"We'd be glad to have you, and we'd enjoy learning more about archeology."

Coy blurted out, "I sure would. I've already decided that I want to be an archeologist when I grow up."

I glared at the little twerp. I couldn't believe he'd said that. I had been waiting for a chance to say the same thing, but now he'd ruined it all. How could I announce my plans to become an archeologist when he'd said it first? I couldn't. It would have made me look like a copy-cat, and that was out of the question.

I decided to take a different approach. "Dr. Montrose, is there anything we could do at the site while you're gone?"

He gave that some thought. "Yes, there is. Maybe you could make some signs and post them on top of that ridge: No Digging or Hunting for Artifacts or something along those lines. At this point, protecting the site is the most important thing."

"We can do that. Spud can weld us some metal signs. Anything else?"

He shook his head and started to say no, but then his face lit up. "You know, there is something else you could do. Yesterday evening at the spring, I noticed that there were several large, half-buried caliche stones showing on the surface. In the night, I woke up thinking . . . those stones are out of context. They shouldn't be there. I saw no evidence of foundation lines that might indicate a house, but I'm curious to know why they are there."

"What could they be?" I asked.

He shook his finger at me. "There, you're already making a mistake. In science, the evidence comes *first* and leads to a conclusion. If you start with a conclusion, you force the evidence to tell you what you want to hear."

"I hadn't thought of it that way. I'm sorry."

He laughed and gave me a pat on the shoulder. "Riley, I hold a doctorate in archeology from Duke University, yet I fight this battle with myself all the time. We all have a tendency to find what we're looking for. You know the old expression, 'I'll believe it when I see it'? That's the way science should function, but so often we reverse that into 'I'll see it when I believe it.' We see what we *think* should be there. That's not good science.

"So here is your assignment. Go to those rocks on the surface of the site, and with a shovel or spade, probe the soil around them. Don't dig. Probe. If your shovel strikes a rock, remove the soil and expose it, then continue probing. If you find several rocks that form a straight line, it might be a foundation. Is that something you boys can do?"

"Yes sir, I think so."

"Excellent. When I come back, we'll already have some of the preparatory work out of the way."

Aaron gave the doctor an admiring glance, and said, "Riley, I think you just got some excellent tutoring in the scientific method. Frank, what you said—'I'll see it when I believe it,'—was one of those gems of wisdom you can think about for a long time."

The doctor shrugged. "Age has a few advantages. Not many, but a few."

The men said their good-byes and climbed up into the Vega, but then Aaron appeared at the door, holding a wooden crate containing books and pamphlets. "Riley, I almost forgot. This is for you boys."

I took the crate. "What is it?"

"Part of Frank's collection on Panhandle archeology."

"Why did you bring it here?"

Aaron gave me one of his mysterious smiles. "Oh, I had a feeling you boys might want to do a little reading."

"You planned this, didn't you?"

"Not at all, not at all."

With one last wave good-bye, Aaron closed the door, and they flew off into the clear blue sky. We watched the plane until it disappeared over the top of Hodges Mesa.

Grampy said, "That Aaron's a pistol. I wish I knew

where he got all his energy. I'd try to bottle it up and sell it . . . after I drank about a gallon of it myself."

At that point, Coy stuck his hand into the crate of reading material. I jerked it away. "Hey, Shorty, that's mine."

"Riley, you don't even like to read."

Mother gave us the cobra eye. "Enough, boys. This is a family project, and I'm sure there will be plenty of reading for all of us. Riley, you can share. Coy, be respectful to your older brother."

Coy and I said, "Yes ma'am," in unison. When Mother looked away, we made faces at each other. Coy stuck out his tongue at me, and I crossed my eyes back at him.

As we walked to the house, Grampy laid a hand on Mother's shoulder. "I thought about what you said last night, Sara Helen. I'd like to go down to Mineral Wells, if you still think it would be all right."

"I think you should. We'll miss you, Daddy, but we'll get along fine. But do you suppose you could come back before winter? I really don't want to feed cattle with Spud all winter, and the boys will be in school."

"That won't be a problem, sugar. At my age, the well goes dry pretty fast." We paused on the porch steps, and Grampy said, "Day after tomorrow, I'll take the train to Fort Worth and leave my truck for you-all. You need some transportation out here, something besides that old wagon."

Mother stared at him in surprise. "We don't drive."

He gave me a sly wink and said, "Well, Riley's done a

little driving you don't know about, and I'll give you a few lessons this afternoon. Driving's not all that hard, and it's time you learned."

Mother wasn't thrilled about learning to drive Grampy's truck. Not only was it noisy, dusty, rough-riding, and uncomfortable, but also I think it embarrassed her to be seen in such a clumsy bucket of bolts. It wasn't ladylike. If she'd been offered the chance to drive Aaron's sleek new Chevrolet sedan, that might have been a different story.

But she realized that Grampy was right: our family needed some kind of motorized transportation, and his truck was all we had. And Grampy was the only teacher available.

It was quite a comedy, watching those two—Mother gripping the wheel with both hands, clenching her teeth, fanning the dust away from her face; and Grampy, the world's worst driving coach, trying his best not to yell at her mistakes. When she clipped a tree with the front bumper, his eyes bulged out, but he didn't say a word.

Somehow it worked out. They didn't kill each other or even come to blows, and by the middle of the afternoon, Mother was driving alone and looking fairly comfortable about it. She still disliked the truck, but she and the vehicle had made an uneasy peace.

Watching her make her solo voyage down the road, Grampy mopped his face with his bandanna. "Well, boys, we have managed to drag your momma into the twentieth century. Maybe we can keep her there for a while." He turned to me. "You're next." He squinted his eyes and looked me up and down. "Son, I think you grew two inches in the night. Unless my eyes are playing tricks on me, you're taller than I am."

We stood back to back and compared our heights. Sure enough, my head was half an inch above Grampy's five foot ten. I was thrilled. "Have I shown you my whiskers?"

"About five times," he grumped. Coy laughed out loud.

When Mother came back in the truck, she climbed out and straightened her hair. "Well, that wasn't as bad as I expected. It might actually be an improvement over a horse and wagon."

Grampy said, "Don't forget: the truck don't eat oats, so you need to put gasoline in the tank every once in a while." He motioned for me to get into the truck. "Let's go, Junior, I'm a-fading fast."

I climbed behind the wheel of the truck, and Grampy took the copilot's seat. I had driven enough on the ranch so that I didn't need the lesson, but Grampy wanted to be sure I was as competent as I thought. We went through the whole process of crank-starting the motor, adjusting the spark and throttle levers, releasing the hand brake, and depressing one of the two foot pedals, one for high speed and one for low speed. I remembered it all.

As we were driving down the road, Grampy said, "Son, when I come back, if that high-speed pedal is worn down to the size of a nickel, I won't be pleased. You don't have to drive this thing wide open all the time."

That made me laugh. "Like you?"

His expression soured. "Uh . . . do as I say, not as I do, Sprout, or you'll be afoot—permanently."

"Yes sir."

On Wednesday, we loaded Grampy's fiddle and leather suitcase into the truck and drove him into Canadian to catch the train. Mother didn't want to drive, but Grampy insisted, saying that she needed the practice. She agreed to do it, if he would promise not to comment on her driving all the way to town. He promised to keep his mouth shut, and he did, though I could see that it wasn't easy for him.

On the station platform, Grampy seemed excited and paced like a racehorse ready to run. When the train was about to pull out, he gave Mother a hug, shook hands with me and Coy, and said, "I'll write when I know where I'll be staying. Boys, take care of my daughter." His eyes misted over, and he hurried up the steps into the Pullman car.

Before leaving town, we bought some groceries and supplies at Gerlach's Store, checked the mail at the post office, bought two fifty-pound blocks of ice at the ice-house, and filled the truck with gasoline. Then we headed back to the ranch. Mother asked me to drive home, which I was more than glad to do.

I noticed that she seemed to be in a quiet mood, and I asked if anything was wrong.

My question jolted her back from her thoughts. "Oh, it's nothing. Saying good-bye is always hard—first Aaron and now Daddy. It leaves a void and reminds me just how isolated we are on the ranch. Sometimes Daddy drives me crazy, but I'm going to miss the old scamp." She forced up a brave smile. "We'll just have to keep ourselves busy, won't we? It's a perfect time for us to learn all we can about archeology, while Dr. Montrose is around to show us what we have on the ranch. He really brings the past to life, doesn't he?"

"He sure does. I'm excited."

"Me too," said Coy, butting into the conversation. When no one responded, he gave us a hangdog look. "Well, gee, can't I be interested too? I can use a shovel just as well as—" He stopped himself when he realized that he had said the wrong word.

Mother perked up. "Speaking of shovels, I'd almost forgotten that you boys have a job to finish."

I glared at Coy. "Big mouth."

It appeared that we would find ourselves back on the chain gang, thanks to Coy, but it didn't turn out that way. When we pulled up in front of the house, we found something that took Mother's mind off of our punishment again.

Chapter 7

A pickup truck was parked in front of the house, and three men in work clothes were sitting on the porch step, waiting for us. We didn't recognize them. Spud came out to meet us and said he wasn't sure who they were or what they wanted, but they had mentioned the name of Aaron Kaplan.

"Aaron?" said Mother. "What on earth?"

We went to the porch and introduced ourselves. The men were a bit grizzled and dusty from work, but polite. The tallest of the three said, "We need to know where you want the telephone, ma'am."

Mother was speechless for a moment. "The telephone! You must be lost."

The man checked to be sure this was the McDaniels ranch, then explained that he and his men had spent the past two days attaching a telephone wire to fence posts, all the way from Aaron's store in Sparrow to our house on the ranch.

You could have knocked us over with a feather. *Aaron was installing a private telephone line to our house!*

When Mother recovered from the shock, she looked at the new telephone. It was a box made of wood, with two bells on the top, a crank on one side, and a black receiver that hung on a metal hook. Inside the box were two dry cell batteries connected to wires. The whole device was designed to be mounted on a wall.

We trooped into the house and Mother chose a spot on the east wall, just behind the kitchen table. The workmen mounted the box to the wall and ran their wire through the attic, then showed us how to use the phone: turn the crank several times and wait for someone to answer on the other end.

Mother served the men some fresh coffee and cookies for their trouble, then they left. The three of us sat at the table, still too shocked to believe what had happened. Aaron was a man full of surprises, but this one topped them all.

"How could he have done this?" Mother said. "How on earth? Why, it must have cost him a fortune."

I said, "Why don't you call him and ask? Let's give it a crank and see if it works."

"You do it, Riley. I'm not sure I'd be coherent. This is just . . . "

I stepped up to the box, lifted the receiver, and gave the crank four or five twirls. I waited for a minute or two. Nothing happened. I had just about decided that the thing wasn't hooked up, when I heard Aaron's voice on the other end.

"Good. It works. What do you think? To whom do I have the honor of speaking on this momentous occasion?"

"Aaron? This is Riley. I'm talking because Mother is too shocked to speak."

He got a good laugh out of that. "Was she surprised?"

"Stunned. We all are. How did you do this?"

"Oh, it wasn't that hard. As your mother pointed out, the primary expense in a commercial phone line comes from the poles and the labor to install them. It occurred to me that all the ranches between your place and Sparrow have mile upon mile of solid cedar fence posts, so why not use them? All it requires is some glass insulators, copper wire, and permission from a few landowners. It happened that a local contractor owed me some money, and he was happy to trade it out with labor."

"But that was sixty miles of wire!"

"Actually, I already had most of it in my warehouse. It came from the auction of a small telephone cooperative in Pratt, Kansas. One of my buyers picked it up last fall. I thought it might come in handy someday."

"Aaron, you amaze me."

He laughed. "The only trouble is that it's a private line and you can't call anyone but me, which might prove frightfully dull, but I'm working on a scheme to patch you into the local telephone exchange. They howled at the idea, but I'll keep working on it. Well, have you finished your book work on archeology?"

"No sir, I haven't begun yet. We just got back from taking Grampy Dawson to the train, but I'll start on it tonight."

"Good, good. I want you to be prepared when Dr. Montrose returns to the site. He's a very busy man, and we're lucky to have him around. Well, put Coy on the line, then I'll chat with your mother."

Coy talked for a while, then handed the phone to Mother. She began by saying, "Aaron, I don't know what to say. I'm flabbergasted." They talked for ten or fifteen minutes.

I felt that Coy and I were intruding into Mother's privacy, so we went out onto the porch. When she came out and joined us, her face had taken on a glow. I guess that having a telephone on the ranch made her feel a bit less isolated than before. Even when we weren't using it, it was sitting on the kitchen wall, a link to the outside world. It was comforting to know that if we needed something, we could call Aaron.

After supper and evening chores, we brought out the crate of reading material and placed it on the kitchen table. I leafed through the journals and glanced at the titles of some of the articles. My enthusiasm for archeology began to fade.

"Mother, these are technical articles, written by doctors and professors. This is a big jump from *Tom Sawyer* and *Treasure Island*. I'm not sure I can read this stuff."

Coy gave his head a nod. Even though he loved to read, and looked professorial in his big glasses, he found the journals rather forbidding too.

I think Mother had the same feeling, but she didn't want to admit it. She pursed her lips in thought. "Boys, Aaron wouldn't have left us this material unless he thought we could get something out of it. Here's what we'll do. I'll read the articles aloud, and you boys take notes. When we're finished, we'll discuss it."

I could feel my lip curling. "Mother, that sounds just like school. This is summer. We're supposed to be on vacation."

She laughed. "Whatever gave you that idea?" She went to the pantry and came back with paper and pencils. "For now, we'll say that this is a trade-off for digging the holes." She sorted through the journals and chose an article called "A Survey of Archeology in the Arkansas River Valley." She sat down and started reading.

The article was exactly twenty-three minutes long. I knew, because I was watching the clock on the wall and counting every tick. I made only one note on my paper: "Snore!" Coy spent his time twisting his hair, chewing his pencil, and making doodles on his page. A heavy silence filled the room when Mother stopped reading.

She laid the journal on the table and said, "Well! That was interesting, wasn't it?"

Silence. I studied the ceiling. Coy continued to doodle.

"Shall we discuss it?"

I said, "Mother, I think I'm going to change my mind about archeology. I'm not as interested as I thought."

Coy muttered, "Yeah, me neither."

"So . . . you want to quit?" she asked. We nodded. "I'm sorry, that's not one of your choices." We groaned. "Boys, we're the caretakers of some important archeological sites on our ranch, and we're going to be good caretakers. Sit up, pay attention, and listen. I'm going to read this article again."

I couldn't believe she was doing this.

But I had to admit that the second time was better, and I even wrote down some notes. Archeology follows rivers. Find water and you'll find evidence of ancient people who clustered there for firewood, wild game, and drinking water. Our Canadian River, the river that carved out the valley in which we lived, was one branch on a vast system of waterways that began in the Rocky Mountains and crossed the Central Plains.

The article said that many advances occurred in the Woodland period, from A.D. 1 to 900. The bow and arrow replaced the spear as a weapon. The first clay pottery appeared, as well as the first signs of gardening. The garden crops held people closer to one place and they began building crude houses, often just a hole in the ground covered with a buffalo hide. The most common arrow point for the Woodland period was the corner-notched Scallorn point.

When Mother read that, my head came up. She said, "That's the arrow point Dr. Montrose found over at Flint Springs, remember? He called it a Scallorn. That's why he thought it was a Woodland site."

"That's right," I said, "and he commented on the lack of pottery. He said that Woodland sites have very little pottery."

She continued reading about the next stage, Plains Village, which spanned the years from 1200 to 1450. The Plains Village economy was equally divided between farming and buffalo hunting, and the increase in farming led to the development of large permanent houses. Along the Washita River in Oklahoma, these structures had post foundations, with roofs of thatched grass. Along the Canadian River in the western Panhandle, the houses were made of stones set vertically in the ground.

Mother looked up from the article. "Those are the sites around Sparrow, the large villages near the Alibates flint quarries. The ones that Aaron said have been plundered."

"Yes," said Coy, nibbling the end of his pencil, "and Dr. Montrose was surprised that Flint Springs wasn't one of those big villages with rock houses. This is starting to make a little sense." He leaned back in his chair and grinned. "Hey, I think I've got this archeology whipped. I'm ready to go back to Flint Springs and start poking around for rocks. We just might uncover a bunch of stone houses."

Mother said, "Well . . . maybe. But it says here that a Woodland house has never been found in the Texas Panhandle."

"So? Let's find the first one. That would be pretty neat."

Mother set the article on the table. "We mustn't get our hopes too high. One article doesn't make us experts, and Dr. Montrose seemed certain that houses aren't there."

"Yes," I said, "but don't forget what else he said: 'I'll see it when I believe it; you find what you're looking for.' I agree with Coy. Let's find the first Woodland house in the Panhandle."

Mother gave that some thought. "Well, why not? There's no sense in dreaming small. But we need to do some more reading about the Woodland period. That will be tomorrow night's assignment."

Chapter 8

The next morning, Coy and I jumped out of our bed-rolls at first light and attended to the morning chores. We helped Spud strain the milk, brought in firewood for the kitchen stove, and straightened up the house.

Spud didn't have any major jobs planned for the day, so I drew out a design for the No Digging signs we planned to post around the Flint Springs site. He said he would have them finished by the afternoon.

By 7:30 Coy and I were ready to drive to Flint Springs, but we had to wait more than twenty minutes on Mother. Even when she wasn't going anywhere special, she took time with her personal appearance. As Grampy had observed, "Your momma ain't very portable. Every time she sits down, she sprouts roots."

Around eight, she came out of her bedroom, looking

fresh and pretty in a long blue dress. Since we would be working outside, she wore long sleeves and a sunbonnet that protected her face from the wind and sun. Women in the Texas Panhandle waged a never-ending battle to keep the skin on their faces and hands from turning to leather. Every morning and night, Mother rubbed something called "coal cream" or "cold cream" on her skin.

We loaded our lunch, a canvas water bag, and three spades into the back of the truck, and Mother let me drive over to the west pasture. I stayed in low gear most of the way, knowing that if I jostled her around too much, Mother would let me know about it.

When we reached the site at Flint Springs, we hardly knew where to begin. When we had looked at it a few days ago, it hadn't appeared very large, but now it did. A two-acre campsite on a six-thousand-acre ranch didn't seem like much country, unless you were trying to find rocks beneath the ground, and then it looked huge.

Dr. Montrose had told us to go to the few rocks that showed on the surface and to start probing around them, so that's what we did. We soon discovered that the ground above Flint Springs had been baked into something like cement by the hot July winds, and we hadn't thought to sharpen our spades on the grinding wheel.

The first problem was, how can you find an underground rock when the ground itself is as hard as a rock? It proved to be impossible. Every time we thought we'd struck a stone and dug out around it, the "stone" proved to be a layer of hard dirt about three inches below the surface. It was very discouraging.

The second problem was that the labor of forcing the blade of a shovel into the ground began to take its toll on our feet. Mother was the first to notice it. She had worn a regular pair of black shoes, which were more fashionable than functional, and after a couple of hours, the instep of her digging foot was beginning to hurt. She parked her shovel, sat down on the running board of the truck, and watched as Coy and I continued the work.

By the time we stopped to eat our lunch, Coy had run out of ambition, and I must admit that I had too. We had worked and sweated all morning and had nothing to show for it. We hadn't found a single buried rock! And the afternoon heat was beginning to close in around us.

We ate in weary silence, then Mother said, "I think I'll let you boys take me back to the house. This is more work than I had expected."

Coy nodded. "Me too. I think Dr. Montrose was right. There aren't any rock houses here."

I didn't have the energy to argue.

We drove back to the house. While Mother and Coy took a nap, I drifted down to the barn and watched Spud gas-weld the signs. He was a thick chunk of a man, powerfully built in the chest, shoulders, and arms, and people often described him as "slow" or "slow-witted." He had been partially deaf since childhood and spoke with a stutter, and he was . . . different. He moved slowly and thought slowly and had a way of working that reminded me of a man underwater.

But you couldn't argue with the results. Spud was a good hand at almost any kind of work, but especially good with metal. Sometimes he used the old-time method of forge welding—heating two pieces of metal red hot in a coal forge and then fusing them together with a hammer and anvil—but for this job he used a method called acetylene welding. He had an acetylene generator that allowed him to cut metal with a torch. Once he had cut the flat pieces of sheet metal, he welded them to steel bars with the torch, using strips of wire as the filler metal.

When Spud worked at skills he had mastered, he was the best, unlike Grampy, who had the patience of a canary. Old Spud would spend all day plodding through a job that would have driven Grampy crazy. And when he had finished welding, grinding, and filing those signs, they were beautiful—as beautiful as a metal sign could be.

I found a quart can of black paint under the workbench and painted the lettering on the signs. NO DIGGING FOR ARTIFACTS! Spud sat nearby on his milking stool, shooing flies with his thick hand and listening while I told him about our failed attempt to find buried rocks at the site. I was never sure that he understood why we were doing it, but after I had finished griping about our big flop at archeology, he said, "Y-you need a pu-pu-pokey rod."

"A what?"

"A pokey rod. I'll m-make you one."

This turned out to be a typical Spud Morris enterprise. He, who was said to be slow-witted, invented and built from junk parts a tool that was perfectly suited for the job. It took him three hours to do it, and I thought he would never get done, but he built me a tool that would penetrate hard ground and locate buried rocks: a pokey rod.

It was beautiful in its simplicity: a steel rod three feet long, with a wooden handle at the top in the shape of a T and the bottom end sharpened on the grinding wheel to a fine point. Putting weight on the handle, you could push the sharpened end as far into the ground as you wanted, and it didn't hurt the instep of your foot.

I told Spud he was a genius, and he thought that was pretty funny, but I was only half joking. He was an absolute master in his little world, and what more could you ask of a genius? I couldn't wait to try out his latest invention.

That night, Mother read us an article called "Woodland Period Occupations in the Texas Panhandle" by a professor at West Texas State Teacher's College in Canyon. I paid close attention and even took some notes.

What I got out of the article was that the Woodland period in the Texas Panhandle was something of a mystery, even to the scholars who had studied it. An abundance of Woodland occupation sites had been found and studied in eastern Oklahoma, Nebraska, southeastern

Colorado, and New Mexico, but very few had been reported along the Canadian River. Woodland people had occupied the Canadian River valley, but they had left very little evidence of structures, only campsites and fire pits without any houses.

No one seemed to know where they had come from or what had become of them. Had they migrated westward from the Caddoan settlements in the east, eastward from the Pueblo settlements in New Mexico, or southward from the Republican River? Had they vanished as a distinct cultural group sometime around A.D. 900, or had they wandered to another place? Or had they evolved into the Panhandle Aspect people who appeared around 1250?

The author raised many questions and gave very few answers. All he could say with any certainty was that two thousand years ago, Woodland people appeared in the valley with bows and arrows and pottery vessels, and sometime around 900 they just disappeared.

It was fascinating! Instead of nodding off to sleep, I found myself wanting to learn more about the subject.

This mysterious group of people came into the Canadian River valley, lived, gave birth to children, hunted buffalo, made pottery vessels out of local clay, and maybe cultivated garden plots. They looked at the stars at night, entertained their children with stories, and laughed at the antics of their camp dogs. They grieved over their departed loved ones and buried them in lonely spots on the prairie. They lived their entire lives without wheels, metal, matches, horses, books, cloth, thread, or soap. And, it seemed, without permanent houses.

And they had done all those things on that windy little hilltop we called Flint Springs, only two miles from the place where I was sitting.

The next morning, Mother gave me permission to drive the truck back over to Flint Springs to put up the signs. I didn't tell Coy about Spud's pokey rod, but invited him to come along. He had suddenly developed an interest in helping Mother can a batch of wild plum jelly, so I went alone. That suited me. If I found some buried rocks, I wouldn't have to share the glory with Mr. Me-Too.

I posted the signs along the edges of the Flint Springs site, then went to one of the surface rocks and began probing with the tool. The difference between the pokey rod and a shovel was astounding, even better than I had hoped. Spud's probe slipped through the compacted soil with very little effort, and on my third or fourth attempt, I felt it strike something solid. I removed the probe and sank it again, a few inches from the original hole. Clunk. That wasn't a small stone or hardpan soil. That was a big rock.

I dropped the probe and went to work with a shovel, and after fifteen minutes of hard digging, found myself looking at the top half of a large caliche boulder, perhaps twelve inches in diameter. Now I had a buried rock in a location where Dr. Montrose had said rocks "shouldn't be."

I began probing around the rock, and before long, struck another solid mass. Grabbing the shovel again, I uncovered the top of another large rock. I drew an imaginary line between the two rocks and extended it to the west, following Dr. Montrose's reasoning that the foundation of a rectangular house would follow a straight line. I probed along the line, going three feet to the west, and was disappointed on finding no rocks. I returned to the first rock and probed a straight line three feet in the other direction, to the east. Again, no rocks.

I took a break, ate an apple, and tried to decide what to do next. Maybe this was nothing but a wild goose chase and I was wasting my time. But then it occurred to me: whatever purpose these big rocks served, maybe they *didn't* follow a straight line. Maybe they formed some kind of cluster instead. I moved away from the straight line and began sinking the pokey rod at random—and struck another rock. When I had removed five inches of soil around it, I had myself another big caliche rock, ten or twelve inches in diameter.

This couldn't be an accident, could it? Rocks that size were abundant at the base of the caprock, where they had broken off and rolled down, but they shouldn't be here on top of the ridge where the soil was free of rock. Dr. Montrose had made that observation. No, someone must have brought the big rocks here, probably rolling them downhill from the base of the caprock.

I continued probing and found more rocks of the same size and at the same depth. By noon, I had uncovered eight of them. Chewing on the biscuits and sausage Mother had packed for my lunch, I walked around and studied the rocks. Up to that point they had seemed to be randomly placed, with no form or shape, but suddenly it occurred to me that what I was seeing wasn't the straight line I had expected, but rather an arc that was part of a *circle*.

Did prehistoric people build circular houses? I tried to remember the articles Mother had read to us and couldn't recall any mention of circular stone houses. I thought of Dr. Montrose's words, "I'll see it when I believe it." I believed that I was looking at part of the foundation of a *circular* house. I wolfed down the rest of my lunch, took a drink of water, and started probing again, this time looking for rocks that would follow the arc I had exposed.

And the rocks were there! Every time I sank the probe, I got that same clunking sound that indicated something big and solid. Once I had figured out the pattern, the rest was simple. All I had to do was dig and hack my way through five inches of hard dirt. I dug like a wild man, like a dog after a bone. I dug until I was exhausted and dripping sweat, stopped for a rest, then dug some more.

By five o'clock that afternoon, I leaned on the shovel and looked down on a circle of rocks twelve feet across:

twenty-eight big caliche boulders that shouldn't have been there . . . but were. There was even a three-foot gap on the east side of the circle that appeared to be a door or other opening.

There was no doubt about it. It had to be a house.

 # Chapter 9

I could hardly wait to get back home to share the news.
I went first to the barn to thank Spud for building me the
pokey rod.

"It's a perfect tool, Spud. You're a genius for sure."

He blushed and mumbled, "Oh g-g-go on." I had
made his day.

I ran up to the house and told Mother and Coy the
news. They were excited too, although Coy was a little
miffed that he had missed out on the discovery. I asked
Mother if it would be all right for me to call Aaron, and
she said I could.

I gave the phone a vigorous cranking, and after several minutes Aaron came on the line. I told him about my
discovery, and he congratulated me on my hard work and
perseverance. Then he said, "Hold on a second. Dr.

Montrose came into town this afternoon for some groceries and supplies, and he's here. I'll let you tell him about it."

The doctor came on the line, and I described what I had found, giving him as many details as I could. He was quiet for a moment. "Well, this is puzzling. What you've described certainly sounds like a structure, but it shouldn't be there. Not only does the site appear to be too old to have permanent structures, but circular architecture has never been reported in the eastern Panhandle. I'm inclined to say that it's some kind of storage feature, but the dimensions you gave are too big for that. Hmm.

"I'm not sure what it is, Riley, but you've found something important. I'm proud of you and anxious to see it. I definitely want to set up some units and do some testing on the site. I'll put together a crew and some equipment and get there as soon as possible. Let's aim for the morning of August first. How does that sound? Are you ready for some serious archeology?"

"Yes sir, I can hardly wait. Should I keep probing and looking for rocks?"

"Oh, absolutely, yes. If there's one structure on that ridge, there might be more. Dig just enough to expose the rocks and leave the rest of the soil undisturbed. The less you dig, the more context you leave for us to study. Good hunting, my boy; keep it up. I'll be seeing you soon."

When I hung up the phone, I turned to Mother and Coy. "Dr. Montrose was impressed."

Coy and I were up early the next morning, itching to get back to the site, but Spud came up to the house around seven and said he needed our help to rebuild some fence. During the night, two of our herd bulls had gotten into a fight and destroyed fifty feet of barbed wire fencing. We had to set five new posts and stretch up all four wires, and it was afternoon before Coy and I left for the site.

When we drove over the crest of the big hill and started down the other side in the west pasture, Coy sat up straight and yelled, "Hey! Somebody's at the site."

His voice startled me so much, I slammed on the brakes. We slid to a stop on the middle of the hill. I looked through the bug-spattered windshield and saw a black Chevrolet truck parked on the hill above Flint Springs. I could see three men walking around.

Coy said, "That couldn't be Dr. Montrose, could it?"

"No, he told me he wouldn't be here until August first."

"Then . . . who? Uh-oh. Riley, you don't suppose they're pot hunters, do you?"

I eased up on the brake pedal, and the truck began to roll down the hill. "I don't know, but I guess we'd better find out."

Coy was getting worried. "What if they don't leave? What'll we do then?"

"Will you stop asking questions and let me think?" The truth was, I didn't have any answers. He gave me a wounded look and sank into silence. We came to the bottom of the hill and turned right onto the trail that led to the site. "Coy, try to put on a brave face. You look like a scared rabbit."

"I am. You heard what Aaron said about pot hunters. They're not very nice people. And don't forget, Grampy's gone."

"Don't you think I know that? Look, they're probably here for a good reason. Surveyors. Maybe they're surveying for a pipeline or something. Don't start off assuming the worst."

I could see that he wasn't convinced, and neither was I. But if they were pot hunters, we couldn't just slink away and let them destroy the site.

I drove up beside their truck and killed the engine. Right away things looked bad. Two of the men had been digging with shovels, right in the center of the rock circle I had exposed! Nearby sat three five-gallon buckets and a wooden device that appeared at first to be a table; only instead of a wooden top, it had a layer of wire mesh. It was a screen.

The third man was walking across the ridge with his eyes to the ground, looking for artifacts.

I glanced at Coy. He looked pale and moon-eyed. I said, "You'd better wait here. There's no sense in advertising that we're nothing but a couple of scared kids." Coy nodded, and I stepped out of the truck.

The two men near the screen leaned on their shovel handles and stared at me as I approached. One of them turned his head and spit some tobacco juice. The third man gave me a glance and kept walking over the site, stooping down to pick up objects on the ground.

I walked over to the men with shovels. One of them had a short, squatty build and was dressed in a T-shirt and greasy overalls, while the other was small, wiry, and dark-skinned.

I gave them a nod and tried to put some steel into my voice. "Afternoon. You men are on private ranch property, and I wondered what you're doing here."

The man in overalls said, "Me and Jaime just work from the shoulders down. You need to talk to Vernon. That's him yonder."

Vernon didn't appear to be the least bit concerned about my presence, as though he were the owner of the land and I was the trespasser.

I turned back to the two men. "Please don't dig any-more. This is a protected archeological—" I suddenly realized that the signs were gone. "What happened to the signs?"

The man shrugged his thick shoulders and grinned at Jaime. "We didn't see no signs."

They had taken down my signs.

I left them leaning on their shovel handles and walked toward Vernon. "Sir? Mister?"

Vernon glanced back over his shoulder and kept walking. "Yeah?"

I quickened my pace and caught up with him. Still, he kept walking.

"What are you doing on our ranch?"

"Looking for arrowheads."

"Sir, this is private property and you don't have permission to be here. And if you're just looking for arrowheads, why are those men digging?"

At last he turned and faced me. He was a man of about forty, tall with a lean, muscular build. He was dressed in dirty jeans and an old felt hat with the brim turned down. His long narrow face was covered with several days' growth of beard, and he had an odd pair of eyes. One of them seemed to be slightly off-center.

He hooked his thumbs into his belt and glared at me. "Permission, huh? Is this one of those ranches where the public ain't welcome?"

"It's private property. We don't allow digging. This site is going to be studied by an archeologist from Boston."

Vernon snorted. "Oh, so it's all right for some big shot Yankee with a college degree, but you won't allow a working man to have a little fun, is that it?"

Somehow he had put me on the defensive, and I didn't know how to respond. I wished that Aaron or Dr. Montrose had been there to do the talking. At last, I blurted out, "Look, this is our land and we don't want you here.

I put up signs and you ignored them. That's trespassing."

Vernon gave me a smirk. "I've never liked signs that tell me I can't do something. Makes me think I'm living in a country where the common people live under the boot of the ruling class. Besides, Sonny, you ain't old enough to own any land, so what gives you the right to tell me what I can and can't do?"

"My mother owns the ranch."

"Oh? Well, send her over and we'll chat. Is she pretty?" The other two men had been listening, and they burst out laughing. That made Vernon grow bolder. "It gets kind of lonesome out here, don't it, Stump?"

"It sure does!" yelled Stump with a bawdy laugh.

Vernon stared at me with his crooked eyes. "Send her over. We'd enjoy the company."

I was so mad, I had begun to tremble. "Are you going to get off our land?"

"That's the wrong question. The question is, can you *make* us get off? And I'm guessing the answer is no. Now, why don't you run along home and bake some cookies with your momma, 'cause if you stick around here, you're liable to get some education they don't offer in school."

I stepped forward, until our noses were only inches apart. *"Stop digging and get off our land."*

His hand moved so rapidly, I didn't see it coming. In a flash, he slapped me across the face so hard that it sent me staggering backward. For a moment, I saw colored spots behind my eyes.

He leveled a finger at me, and behind the finger was a face twisted with meanness. "Don't get into the face of a man unless you're ready to back it up with something besides your mouth. You need to learn a few manners before you get yourself hurt. Now, clear out of here. We ain't hurting your precious ranch, and we ain't leaving till we're good and ready."

My voice was trembling when I said, "I'll leave, mister, but I'll be back."

Chapter 10

As I walked back to the truck, I heard the men laughing and talking behind me. Stump congratulated Vernon on the job he'd done on me, and Vernon snarled, "I hate a mouthy kid."

Coy was waiting in the truck, pale and bug-eyed. As we drove away, he said, "That man slapped you!" He pointed to the right side of my face, which was beginning to sting. "And you're getting a black eye."

I wasn't surprised. He'd hit me with an open hand, but there had been plenty of power behind it. I could feel the swelling around my right eye.

"What are we going to do?" Coy muttered.

"You'll see. And please don't chatter. I'm not in the mood for it." I was so filled with anger, I could hardly talk. There was only one thing on my mind.

As we approached the house, Coy spotted a car out front. "Riley, someone's at the house."

"I don't care."

I left the truck running and got out. On my way to the house, I passed the car, a black Dodge Brothers sedan. I had a feeling I had seen it before, but my mind was in a fog and I couldn't remember where. Then, when I breezed through the yard gate, I saw two pretty redheaded girls sitting on the porch, playing a card game.

As I neared the porch, they looked up and smiled. "Hello, Riley."

They were Laura Higgins's little sisters, Rachel and Sally. Any other time, I would have been glad to see them. Not only were they sweet little girls, but they had an older sister who was even nicer and prettier than they were. But today, I wished they hadn't dropped in for a visit.

I entered the house and let the screen door slam behind me. Mother hated the noise of the screen door slamming and had scolded Coy and me about it many times.

She was sitting at the kitchen table with Laura and Mrs. Higgins. Mother's head snapped up at the slamming of the screen, and her eyes bored into me. "Riley? What's wrong?" She saw my swollen eye and rushed toward me. "What on earth . . ."

I gave her a quick summary of what had happened. "I'm going back over there, Mother, and I'm taking the shotgun. I won't let them come onto our ranch and destroy that site, the idiots."

I started toward the closet where we kept the gun, but Mother blocked my path. "Riley, no. Sit down and cool off."

"I don't want to sit down and cool off. I'm going to get those apes off our land even if I have to—"

She stamped her foot on the floor. "Riley McDaniels, I am still your mother! The Bible says, 'Children, obey your parents.' Now sit down and let me get a cold cloth for your face."

The room was as still as a tomb. Coy and the girls had followed me into the house and were standing in the doorway. Laura and Mrs. Higgins sat frozen at the table, staring up at me. Everyone seemed to be holding their breath, waiting to see what would happen next.

I was angry and humiliated, but not so much that I was willing to disobey my mother. I sank down in a chair, while Mother dashed to the sink for a wet cloth. Laura and Mrs. Higgins seemed embarrassed to be caught in the middle of a family crisis, and Mrs. Higgins said they probably should be going.

"No, please stay," I said. "There's no need to rush off. I'm sorry about all this. I'll be all right. Coy, I guess you'd better shut off the truck. Can you do it?"

He nodded. "I think so. Push the spark lever all the way up?"

"That's right. Thanks."

Mother told me to lean my head back, and she placed the cool, wet cloth over my face. It seemed to help take away some of the pain. As I began to relax, my anger slipped away like air leaving a balloon. I felt weak and noticed that my legs were trembling.

Mother returned to her chair. "Who were they?"

"I don't know, Mother. I'd never seen them before. They looked like riffraff, the kind Aaron told us about—men who dig up graves and sell the artifacts."

"The nerve of that man, to strike you on your own land!"

Mrs. Higgins bobbed her head. "I've never heard of anything so brazen. You'd think we didn't have any laws in this country."

Mother said, "I wish Daddy were still here."

I removed the compress. The eyes of the ladies went to my face. I could tell from their reactions that I had a pretty good shiner. I said, "Well, Grampy's gone and that's too bad, but I'm still here. We promised Dr. Montrose that we would protect the site. Those goons are over there destroying the house I found, and the longer we sit here, the more damage they'll do. I could take Spud with me."

Mother shook her head. "Riley, you're a very contentious young man and you have a strong sense of right and wrong. I've always admired that about you, but this is a time for cool heads and clear thinking."

"Mother . . ."

"If those men live on the margins of the law, don't you suppose they'll have guns? I'm not ready to sacrifice you for science, no matter how noble it is. If you went over there with a gun, it would be very foolish behavior."

I had to admit she was right. "Okay, I agree, but we can't just sit around doing nothing."

"Why don't you try to call Aaron? He'll know what to do."

I had forgotten about the telephone. I sprang from my chair and cranked the phone. It was answered by one of Aaron's clerks at the store. I returned to my chair. "He's gone for the day."

Laura had been silent through all this, but now she said, "This might sound obvious, but what about the sheriff?"

Mother said, "We can't call Canadian on this telephone." She glanced up at the clock on the wall. "And as late as it is, by the time we drove into town and he drove back out here, it would be dark."

"We have a phone at our house," said Laura. "If Riley loped up the canyon horseback, he could be there in half an hour."

We all agreed that was a good idea. I asked Laura where the phone was located in the house. She told me, and proceeded to explain that you had to lift this "black thing" out of "another black thing that's shaped like a fork, but be sure both wires are connected to the battery, because sometimes one of them comes loose and—"

Mrs. Higgins gave her head a shake. "Laura, why don't you just ride with him. You could be there in the time it takes to explain that contrary thing. But come straight back."

As Laura and I were leaving the house, Coy came up to me. "Riley, I wouldn't mind going along for the ride. It might be—"

"No."

"—fun. Please?"

"No, Coy. It'll be a hard ride, and you wouldn't enjoy it."

His face fell. "Then I'll have to stay here and play Old Maid with those girls."

"Maybe next time."

Laura and I went down to the barn to whistle up the horses. I rattled the feed bucket, and they came galloping in from the pasture. Dolly, my little mare, was the first into the corral and, as usual, she had her ears pinned back and was ready to bite the other horses away from the feed. We caught two horses: Dolly for Laura and Snips for me. I thought Laura might enjoy riding my mare. Snips was the big red dun gelding Grampy Dawson rode when he was at the ranch. He was a good, gentle horse, but I had never particularly enjoyed riding him. He lacked the fire and quick action of Dolly, and when I was on his back I felt as though I were riding a lumber wagon.

Grampy had left his saddle in the barn, and I cinched it up on Dolly. I figured the stirrups would be about the right length for Laura and that turned out to be correct, so I didn't have to relace the stirrup leathers.

Passing the house, we waved good-bye to Mother and Mrs. Higgins. Coy was sitting on the step with his chin resting on both hands. He watched us with a glum expression while one of Laura's sisters dealt the cards.

Beyond the house, we gave the horses their heads and loped north into the upper end of Picket Canyon. Now and then we had to slow down for rocks and heavy brush, but for the most part, it was a fast trip. Once we had climbed the caprock out of the canyon, we were on flat prairie country and we made even better time.

When we reached the Higgins place, Laura rang up the central operator at the telephone company office in Perryton and asked to be connected to the Hemphill County sheriff's office. Since this was a long-distance call, it took the operator several minutes to make the connection. When Sheriff South came on the line, Laura handed me the receiver.

The sheriff had a kind of squeaky voice, and he sounded impatient. Hearing his voice, I formed a mental picture of Jake South: a shriveled old man in an oversized felt hat, sitting at his desk in the basement of the courthouse, leaning on his elbows and barking into the telephone.

I told him the story about the pot hunters trespassing on our land. The line was silent for a moment, then he said, "They're hunting arrowheads?"

"Well, yes sir, but they're also digging on the site, and as I mentioned—"

"Son, half the people in this county hunt arrowheads. It's not exactly a crime. I've got a cigar box full of 'em myself."

"Sir, this is an important archeological site, and they're trespassing."

"Well, thunder, let Abner Dawson handle it."

"Sheriff, Grampy went down to Mineral Wells to play his fiddle. We don't know when he'll be back."

"That figures," the sheriff grumbled. "Well, you called on a bad day. Mrs. Hefley got into her husband's homemade wine and passed out on Main Street; drove her car right through the south wall of the train depot."

"Really? Was she hurt?"

"No, she wasn't hurt, just drunker than Cooter Brown, but we've got a car sitting in the middle of the depot, and the railroad people are raising holy Ned. There's no way I can make it out to your place today or tomorrow, and maybe not even the next day."

"Three days?"

"And if you ask me, it's a bunch of foolishness anyway. Let 'em collect a few arrowheads and they'll leave. If they ain't gone in two days, call me back."

"Sheriff, it's not just the arrowheads. They're digging up an important . . . hello? Sheriff South?" He had hung up. Laura was waiting for my report. "He's not coming. He says he's got too much to do in town, but I think he just doesn't want to drive all the way out here. He doesn't understand about archeology. Nobody around here does."

"I'm sorry," she said.

We mounted up and started the journey back home. Riding up to Laura's house, we had put a heavy sweat on the horses, and now we let them move at a more leisurely pace. Laura said, "When did you get so interested in archeology? I've never heard you mention it before."

I told her about Dr. Montrose's visit, the work I'd done exposing rocks at the Flint Springs site, and the reading Coy and Mother and I had been doing at night. I gave her a quick lesson on Panhandle archeology and explained the difference between archeology and collecting arrowheads as a hobby.

Down in the canyon, we stopped our horses beneath the shade of a big hackberry tree. Laura had been listening with keen interest. "My, my," she said, "you've become quite the scholar. You've never shown that kind of interest in schoolwork."

"Archeology is different; it's more than dry facts on a page. When you pick up a flint tool or a piece of pottery, you're holding something that was made a thousand or two thousand years ago, by someone who lived on this very ranch. It makes me want to know more about those people."

"That's fascinating, Riley. I'm beginning to understand why you got so mad. They're destroying something that can't be replaced."

"That's right, and they're too dumb to know it."

"You said the professor is coming back to do an excavation?"

I nodded. "That's what he said—if there's anything left."

"Would you mind terribly if I came over and took part?" I swung my gaze around and stared at her. For a moment I couldn't speak, and I guess she took it the wrong way. She looked away and said, "Oh, never mind; it's not important."

"Laura, I think that would be great!"

She brightened and looked at me with those blue eyes that reminded me of a deep pool of springwater. "Honestly? You wouldn't think it was awkward, having a girl around?"

"Not at all. No. Absolutely not. I'm just surprised that you'd be interested. It's hard, dirty work."

"Surely we can come up with a bar of soap and a bucket of water." A shadow passed over her face. "But I'll have to talk Mother into letting me go, and that won't be easy. She's very protective, you know."

"Just tell her you'll be with me."

She studied me for a long moment. A smile fluttered at the corners of her mouth, like a butterfly trying to get out of a box. "I don't think you understand mothers very well, and we need to get back to the house, before she sends out a posse."

"A posse? What are you talking about?"

"We'd better hurry, that's all. I don't want Mother to worry." She gave Dolly her head, and they went loping down the canyon in a flash of red hair and blue cotton cloth. I sat there for a moment, watching her, then thumped Old Lumber Wagon in the sides and tried to catch up.

Chapter 11

Both mothers were on the porch when we rode up to the house. Mrs. Higgins stood at stiff attention and had one hand resting on her brow, shading her eyes from the sun. She was gazing off in the distance like a ship's captain looking for land. When we came riding up, I could see relief on her face.

We left the horses tied to the fence and went up to the porch. Laura and her mother exchanged some kind of secret message with their eyes, and my mother whispered, "You should have been back twenty minutes ago."

"We got back as soon as we could. I guess we were talking about archeology and weren't watching the time."

Mother nodded. "Well, what did the sheriff say?" When I told her, she seemed annoyed but not surprised. "I think Sheriff South needs to retire. He's been a good sheriff, but there comes a time when a man should step aside for someone younger. What are we supposed to do now? Do you think it would do any good if I went over to the spring and talked to those men?"

"No, they're not the kind of men who show much respect for a lady. Mother, Spud and I could—"

She cut me off with a raised finger.

Mrs. Higgins said they needed to start for home so that her husband wouldn't worry that they'd had car trouble on the way. Even though our houses were only five straight-line miles apart, there was no decent road through the canyons. You had to take a circuitous route and follow the only road that climbed up the caprock. When you drove between our houses, the distance stretched into seventeen miles and took most of an hour.

Mrs. Higgins left Mother with a sack of fresh okra from her garden, and Mother gave her two jars of her wild plum jelly.

We walked them to their car, and I found myself beside Laura. I said, "If Dr. Montrose still wants to do the excavation, I'll let you know the date and time." I opened the door for her. "But if I go to the trouble of riding all the way to your house, I hope I won't find you and Jackie Tinsley sitting in the porch glider."

Jackie was one of our classmates at Notla School, and had shown more than a casual interest in Laura.

She raised one eyebrow. "Well, you never know. His family has a lot of money, and Daddy says we should never hold that against a fellow."

I felt my temper rising. "Laura, I really don't think—"

She stepped into the car and closed the door. She smiled at me through the window, and her lips formed the words, "I'm just teasing." Then she rolled down the glass. "Thanks for letting me ride your mare."

When the car pulled away from the house, I realized that Coy was standing beside me. "What were you two whispering about?"

"Coy, if you must know, we were discussing the Mississippi River. Did you know that it floods every spring and deposits huge amounts of silt at the mouth?"

His eyes rolled up inside his head and he groaned. "Riley, you are the biggest liar I ever met! If you were talking about the Mississippi River, I'll eat your shoe."

I started toward the house. "What we were talking about is none of your business, but you can be sure it wasn't about you."

"I don't appreciate you leaving me behind. I can ride a horse as well as Laura can."

"Oh sure. You get saddle sores just looking at a horse. Besides, you had those two girls all to yourself, so what's your complaint?"

Coy glanced over his shoulders to make sure Mother wasn't listening. "Those are the silliest girls I ever met."

"You didn't enjoy playing Old Maid?"

"Riley, I hate that game. And you know what they played after that? Hospital. They wanted me to be a wounded soldier just back from France, so they could be nurses."

"I'll bet that was fun."

He stared at me through the lenses of his glasses. "Are you crazy? I quit and played with the dog. You know, we're lucky we don't have any sisters. Can you imagine having girls around the house all the time? They're so peculiar."

I got a chuckle out of Coy's fuming. He had a point about girls, but I didn't want to tell him so.

After we finished the evening chores, Mother said I could try to call Aaron again. It was around seven o'clock when I cranked the phone. This time, he was there. After I told him about the diggers in the west pasture, his voice dropped into a serious tone.

"I see. Mencken called such creatures 'gaping bipeds.'"

"*Gaping bipeds?*" My mind formed a picture of a hairy ape-man, staring with his mouth open. I had to laugh. "That's a great description, but who's Mencken?"

"H. L. Mencken. He edits a journal called *American Mercury* and writes with the sting of a scorpion. I don't always agree with his politics, but his prose is delightfully wicked. You should read his descriptions of President Coolidge. Oh, by any chance, did you write down the license plate number of that truck in the pasture?"

"No sir, I didn't even think of it." I turned to Coy. "You didn't write down their license number, did you?"

"No, but I memorized it." Trying to hide my surprise, I handed him the phone. "Aaron? This is Coy. Hi. It was a Texas plate, HC315. Oh, thanks. Bye." Wearing a triumphant little smirk, Coy handed the phone back to me.

Aaron said, "Riley, let me make a few calls. I'll get back to you within the hour."

I hung up the phone and turned to my little brother. "How did you happen to memorize the license plate number?"

"Oh, I figured it might come in handy. That's what they do in all the detective books. I'm surprised you didn't think of it."

"I had other things on my mind. How did you remember the number?"

Coy studied his fingernails and put on a show of being nonchalant. "Those of us with natural detective skills just notice those things, I guess."

"Hurry up and tell me."

"Okay." He smiled. "I'll reveal my secret. *HC* is Hutchinson County. Sparrow is in Hutchinson County, right? Three/fifteen is the month and year I was born. HC315. Now admit that you're impressed."

"I'll admit that you were lucky. Anyone could remember a tag number that had his birth date on it."

Coy drew himself up like a snake. "Yeah, but you have to *look* at the tag to begin with, and that's more than you did."

"If my birthday had been on the tag, I would have noticed. You were just lucky."

Coy turned to Mother, who was reading in her chair by the window. "Mother, Riley won't admit that I'm more observant than he is."

Mother's eyes came up from her book. She rose from the chair, walked to the hall closet, and returned to her chair—wearing a pair of earmuffs. She went back to reading her book and ignored us.

I had to laugh. That was a new and creative response to our bickering, and she looked pretty funny, wearing earmuffs in the middle of summer.

True to his word, Aaron called back an hour later. "His name is Vernon McElroy and he's a certified bad guy: bootlegging, assault, theft. And get this: he served as a city policeman in Sparrow for six months. I've probably crossed paths with him before. Oh, and there's an outstanding warrant for him in Lubbock County for car theft."

"How did you learn all that?"

"I'm the mayor of Sparrow, Riley. I have connections. Do you know if they're camped in the pasture?"

"No sir. Do you want me to check?"

"Absolutely not. Stay away from them. My guess is they'll be there overnight. Looting takes time, even for men who are good at it. Now listen. Be around the house at ten o'clock tomorrow morning and have Abner's truck ready to go. Oh, and make sure there aren't any cows standing in the road."

"You're going to fly over here?"

"Yes, and I'll have the sheriff with me."

"I wouldn't be too sure about that. When I talked to him, he didn't seem the least bit interested in our problems."

"You just have to use the right approach. How's your mother?"

I glanced at her and smiled. "Well, at the moment she's reading a book and wearing earmuffs so she won't have to listen to me and my little brother arguing."

He roared at that. "Good solution. Put her on the line and I'll say hello. I'll see you in the morning."

At 9:55 the next morning, we heard the drone of an airplane in the distance. Moments later, Aaron's Vega flew a pass down the road, checking for cows, then landed from the north, into the wind. He taxied the plane to the house and shut off the engine. The door opened and there was Aaron, looking fresh and exuberant in a starched white shirt and plaid vest.

He hopped down to the ground and gave a hand to his passenger, Sheriff Jake South, whose face had acquired the greenish color of spoiled cheese. Aaron explained that the air had been a little choppy between Canadian and the ranch, and that this had been the sheriff's first experience in a flying machine.

Sheriff South greeted us with the briefest of nods. I couldn't tell if he was irritated at us for interrupting his day or if he was merely sick. When he lurched around to the other side of the plane and launched his breakfast onto the ground, I decided it was a combination of both.

Aaron smiled, then gave me a lingering glance. "Your black eye?"

"Vernon."

He nodded and tightened his lips.

While the sheriff was occupied, Aaron explained how he had coaxed him into coming to the ranch. "I asked if he owned a dog and he said that he did, a bloodhound. Bloodhounds eat a lot. I happened to have a thousand pounds of bagged dog food in my warehouse, so we worked a little trade. And flying in the Vega, he didn't have to drive over thirty miles of bad road. He has a bad back, you know." We heard the sheriff behind the plane. "I didn't think about him getting airsick."

Mother was astounded. "What were you doing with a thousand pounds of dog food? You don't even own a dog."

"It sold for two dollars at an auction. I've had it in my warehouse for six months and had just about decided I might have to eat it myself."

We all stared at him in wonder. Mother said, "Sometime I'd like to see this warehouse of yours. It must be as full as Fibber McGee's closet."

Aaron smiled, and his gaze slid toward the horizon. "It's large and it's full. Most people buy something when they need or want it. I buy when the price is right. Later, I find a use for it."

After a few moments, the sheriff joined us. His face had changed color, from green to gray. He carried his big black felt hat and mopped his face with a red bandanna. He turned his grumpy glare on me. "Well, you got me out here. Let's get started. I still have problems in town."

Chapter 12

To no one's surprise, Aaron had worked out a plan. I would drive the sheriff over to Flint Springs in Grampy's truck. I was to stay in the truck while the sheriff arrested the men and put them in handcuffs. If all went well, we would load them into the back and drive them to the jail in Canadian.

In case the men tried to make a run for it, Aaron would be circling overhead in the Vega. It wasn't clear exactly what he planned to do in that event, but I was sure he had something in mind. He always did.

Aaron glanced down at the sheriff's waist. "You're not going to carry a sidearm?"

"No sir. Never have and don't intend to start now. If I can't arrest three arrowhead hunters without a gun, I'll turn in my badge. Let's go."

Aaron shrugged and started toward the plane. Mother followed him. "Aaron, would you mind if Coy and I rode with you? We don't want to stay here and miss all the excitement."

"There might be more than you'd like. The air's pretty rough this morning."

"Bring it on," she said, and stepped up into the plane. Aaron caught my eye and gave me a look of surprise. I was surprised too.

As we drove toward the west pasture, the sheriff rode in stiff, stony silence, glaring at the road with eyes that peered out beneath a hedge of shaggy brows. The silence made me uneasy, so I said, "Well, how's your dog?"

"What frog?"

"No, your *dog*. Your bloodhound."

"Oh." He stuck a finger into his left ear and twisted it around. "Well, Colonel's been bad. He's started digging out of his kennel at night, going out and killing skunks. He left one on the front porch the other night, and the wife liked to have had a stampede." His eyes tightened on me. "Son, what is it about this ranch that draws crooks? This makes the second time I've been out here in two months."

"I don't know, Sheriff. We just try to mind our own business."

"There's eight hundred taxpayers in this county, and only fifteen of 'em live on this side of the river. I can't be running out here every other week."

That was the end of the conversation.

When we crested the hill that lay between the two pastures, I could see the pot hunters' truck, still parked above Flint Springs, and three men digging beside a mound of dirt. I glanced at the sheriff to see if he was getting nervous. His expression hadn't changed.

Overhead, Aaron's plane cleared the top of the mesa and began circling the spring, while I eased the truck down the west slope of the hill. Suddenly the trespassers sprang into action, dashing around and tossing tools into the back of their truck, as though the appearance of a vehicle and an airplane at the same time had alerted them to what was coming. They dived into the cab of the truck and sped across the pasture toward the two-rut trail that led off our ranch and down to the river road.

I glanced at the sheriff. "They're going to make a run for it."

"Try to head 'em off. Get in front of 'em."

"Okay. Hang on."

I let the truck coast faster down the hill. The road was still rutted from spring rains and littered with big rocks, and the truck bounced so high I thought we might be thrown out. The sheriff gripped the door with one hand and the bottom of his seat with the other.

"Son, you'd better cob this thing or they'll get in front of us!"

"Speed up?"

"Heck yes, speed up! Hurry!"

We went careening down the hill. I was terrified. Driving alone, I never would have come off that hill at such a high rate of speed, but these were unusual circumstances. I gripped the steering wheel with both hands and somehow kept the truck on the road, between a ravine on the left and a dirt bank on the right.

We made it to the bottom of the hill. I pressed down on the high-speed foot pedal, slid around a curve, and saw a straight empty road up ahead. The crooks hadn't gotten there yet, so we still had a chance of—

Suddenly the truck burst into view in front of me, coming out of the pasture to my right. I slammed on the brake pedal and barely avoided hitting them broadside. Vernon was driving, and I caught a glimpse of his face as he turned hard to the right and slid into the road. His jaws were clenched and his eyes gave me a menacing glare.

The crooks sped south down the road. They were ahead of us now. I glanced at the sheriff. "What now?"

"Stay on their tail." He studied me with his smoky gray eyes. "Son, are you old enough to be driving this thing?"

"No sir. Do you want to drive?"

"It's too late for that. Try not to get us killed."

Vernon was driving like a wild man, flying over high spots in the road and rattling the axles when the truck came back to earth, leaving a trail of buckets and shovels in the road behind him. I didn't dare swerve to avoid them, just smashed my way through.

The truck was pulling away from us. Two more miles and they would reach the river road. Once they hit the smoother ground, they would be gone.

Out of the corner of my eye, I caught sight of a blue shadow swooping down from the sky. It was Aaron's Vega, scraping the tops of the mesquite bushes. As he approached Vernon's truck, something came flying out the window . . . a white object. It landed on the hood, and suddenly the truck disappeared in a white cloud.

Astonished, I glanced at the sheriff. "Was that a *bomb?*"

The sheriff arched his shaggy brows in surprise. "Two-pound sack of flour. He had ten of 'em on the plane. I wondered why."

Flour! Who but Aaron would have thought of that? Well, it sure worked. Blinded by the flour cloud, Vernon and his truck jumped a ditch on the left shoulder, tore the left front wheel completely off the axle, and scraped to a stop in the middle of a sage-covered sand hill.

I drove up to the rear of the truck and stopped. We could hear the men coughing and shouting. Overhead, Aaron gained altitude, banked the Vega, and circled back around for another run.

I waited for the sheriff to jump out and make his arrests. Instead, he sat and watched as Aaron dropped the nose of the plane and came in for a second pass. Out came another sack of flour, as the Vega roared overhead not more than fifty feet above us. I could actually feel the vibration of the engine. The sack hit the truck broadside and exploded, engulfing it in another cloud of white powder.

I noticed that the sheriff was yielding to an impulse to smile. "Well, I'll be jiggered. Kaplan always struck me as kind of a smarty-pants, but he does good work, don't he? Never would have thought of it myself, bombing crooks with flour." He actually chuckled a few times.

The Vega banked, circled, and came back for another run. From somewhere in the cloud, we heard a man cry out, "No more! Calf rope, we surrender. We quit! Call 'im off or he'll kill us all!"

"Well, come on out!" the sheriff yelled. "Hands up. I want to see the hair in your armpits."

A moment later, the three men stumbled out of the cloud, their hands high in the air. They were covered from head to foot with flour and resembled creatures from another galaxy. Aaron's plane was bearing down on us again, but when he saw the men with their hands in the air, he pulled up and wagged his wings as he passed over us.

The sheriff stepped out of the truck. Our rough ride must have bothered his back, as he took his first few steps hunched over like a turkey. He grunted and groaned, straightened himself up, and said to the men, "Turn around, you codfish; hands behind your backs. You're going to the Crossbar Hotel."

The men did as they were told. The sheriff walked down the line, snapping handcuffs on their wrists. Stump said, "What's the charge? We was only hunting arrowheads."

"Well, that was pretty dumb, wasn't it? You got caught, and now I'll ship you down to Lubbock County. They want to talk to you boys about borrowing cars."

Stump hung his head and said no more. With the Vega still circling above us, the sheriff told the men to load up into the back of Grampy's truck. Vernon walked up to me and growled, "I should have smacked you a few more times, sonny."

"Maybe you should have."

"Stool pigeon."

I returned his glare and said, "Thief. Looter. Vandal."

"You're lucky I'm wearing cuffs, you little jerk."

"And you're lucky Aaron Kaplan's up in that airplane, you gaping biped, or he'd box your ears off."

The sneer on Vernon's mouth went flat. "That was Kaplan? From Sparrow?" He turned toward his friend. "Hey, Stump, that's Kaplan up there."

Stump gave his head a shake. "I told you we should have stayed out of that."

I didn't understand what he meant until later.

The men climbed into the back of the truck and we started back to the house. I was looking forward to getting them off the ranch.

Aaron had already landed the plane by the time we

arrived. He was standing with a hand resting on the left wing, swigging a glass of Mother's tea. He looked as calm and fresh as if he'd spent the morning in a sidewalk cafe. When we got out of the truck, he lifted his glass in a salute and said, "Well done, Sheriff."

Sheriff South straightened up his back and said, "And I didn't need a gun, did I?"

I asked Mother if she'd enjoyed the plane ride. She said, "It was a little scary when we were pruning the mesquite trees, but Aaron's a very good pilot."

"Where do you suppose he got the idea for flour bombs?"

"He did it during the war."

I stared at her. "He dropped sacks of flour on the Germans?"

"That's what he said." She glanced at Aaron and spoke loudly enough so that he could hear. "I'm no longer shocked by his tales. Most of them turn out to be true."

Aaron dipped his head in appreciation.

I had supposed that Aaron or I would have to drive the sheriff and the men all the way into Canadian, but Sheriff South's back had taken such a beating, he asked Aaron to fly them back to town. Aaron said he didn't mind, and in fact, he needed to fuel up the Vega. He said the plane would hold six passengers, and there was one open seat left. He wondered if any of us—Coy, Mother, or I— wanted to go along for the ride.

Mother said she'd had enough adventure for one

afternoon and volunteered to stay at the house. That left the open seat for me or Coy. We had to settle it with a flip of a coin, and Coy lost. It made him so mad, he could hardly speak. Out came his lower lip, and he stomped into the house, muttering that I had cheated him.

I was shocked. It had been perfectly honest and fair: "Heads I win, tails you lose."

Aaron let me ride up front with him, so I got to watch him go through his preflight checklist. Once we got airborne and leveled out at five thousand feet, he even let me take the controls, although he kept his hands on the yoke.

Flying an airplane! It was the fulfillment of every boy's dream.

Chapter 13

In Canadian, we discharged the passengers and I told Aaron about the conversation I'd heard between Stump and Vernon. "They seem to know you better than you know them."

He shook his head. "I can't place them. Wait!" He walked over to Stump. "You were a city policeman in Sparrow, working for Joe McGreggor?"

Stump gave him a mournful look and nodded. "It was me and Vern that bagged you that night on the street and—"

"Shut up, Stump!" Vernon yelled.

Stump ignored him. "—and chained you up in the Oasis Hotel. McGreggor made us do it. I'm sorry, Mr. Kaplan. It was a stupid thing to do."

Vernon remained unrepentant to the end. Curling his lip at Aaron, he snarled, "You'll get yours one of these days. There's still plenty of men around this country who'd bump you off for the price of a soda pop."

Aaron laughed. "Yes? Well now, it's not likely to be you."

Sheriff South had made the return flight without getting sick and seemed in a fairly jolly mood. He said he would send a mechanic out to the ranch to tow Vernon McElroy's truck back to town, and we could keep any artifacts the men had taken from the site.

I said, "You won't need them as evidence?"

"Nope. Those fellers will be on their way to Lubbock first thing in the morning. Let the taxpayers of Lubbock County feed 'em."

We fueled up the Vega and landed back at the ranch around four o'clock. We gathered Mother and Coy, loaded up in the truck, and began the grim task of surveying the damage the crooks had done to the Flint Springs site. Mother rode up front with Aaron, and Coy and I rode in the back.

Coy was still sulking. "You cheated on the coin flip."

"Coy, I borrowed the coin from Aaron. It was a regular nickel. How could I have cheated?"

"I don't know, but you did. You couldn't be that lucky."

I laid a hand on his shoulder. "I know you must be very upset. I understand."

He jerked away. "Don't touch me, you swindler." He was hilarious when he got mad.

But there was nothing funny when we reached the site. The damage was even worse than we had imagined. Vernon and his pals had dug a crater three feet deep and five feet across, right in the center of the house. They had cut the heart out of it, leaving a heap of ruins: piles of screened dirt, hundreds of burned rocks and flint chips. They had even dug out the foundation rocks and tossed them into a heap, obliterating the outline of the house.

If they had set out to destroy the site out of sheer malice, they couldn't have done a better job. At first I was enraged at this act of senseless vandalism, but as the minutes stretched into half an hour, my anger changed to gloom. It depressed me to think that there were people in the world who could destroy part of mankind's memory without giving it a thought, without a hint of remorse.

It didn't improve my mood when Aaron said, "You know, under Texas law, this isn't even illegal. All you can do about this is file on them for trespassing."

Mother moved her gaze across the wreckage. "Is there anything Dr. Montrose can do with what's left?"

Aaron shook his head. "I don't think so. All the information, the soil profiles, the depth of the deposits, the location of the artifacts, the relationship between tools and scraps of bone, the traces of food that might have been left on the floor of the house"—he pointed to the piles of screened dirt.—"are over there, all mixed up. I doubt that he'll want to come back. He was so excited that you'd found a circular house. It would make him sick to see this."

Mother nodded and started walking back to the truck. The rest of us followed, like mourners in a graveyard. Aaron was walking a few steps in front of me, and I noticed that he paused for a moment and looked down at the face of a large rock that was barely visible in the grass and broom weed. He ran the toe of his boot over it and walked on to the truck.

From there, Aaron drove us over to the south end of the pasture, where Vernon's crippled truck had come to rest. We got out and walked over to it. The door on the right side had been bashed in, and there was a perfect impression of a bag of flour on the hood. The whole inside of the cab was covered with a layer of white powder.

We had come to retrieve the artifacts the men had taken from the site, and we found them in a gunnysack. Aaron poured the contents out on the running board: ten nice Scallorn arrow points, three dart points, seven end scrapers, two flint drills, and twelve shards of thick pottery.

Aaron shook his head. "They didn't even find anything worth selling."

"What were they looking for?" Mother asked.

"Oh, complete pots, beads made of turquoise or shell, grave goods—the sort of things you'd find in a Plains Village house. Those crumbs were so ignorant, they didn't know they were digging in the wrong place.

A Woodland house would be of tremendous interest to an archeologist, but worthless as a source of black market treasures. Woodland people weren't prosperous. They didn't have many trinkets."

Coy said, "But surely there's *something* Dr. Montrose can use."

"I doubt it, Coy. Those are nice artifacts, but they don't tell him anything he doesn't already know. We have tools without a context. The information value is zero."

I said, "I guess we can forget about the excavation."

"So it appears." Aaron noticed the pokey rod in the back of our truck. He picked it up and looked at it. "What is this?"

When I told him, he nodded and said no more.

We loaded into the truck and started the three-mile drive back to the house. The sun was settling down on the horizon, and the evening shadows grew long, mirroring the shadows that had fallen over our thoughts. Coy and I rode in silence. He had forgotten that he was mad at me, and I had lost my appetite for teasing him.

We were both surprised when, instead of driving up the long hill that lay between the west pasture and the mesa pasture, Aaron turned off onto the trail that led back to the Flint Springs site. When he parked the truck near the screen piles, Coy called out, "What are we doing back here?"

Aaron stepped out and picked up the rod. "I want to check something."

We followed him to the single rock he had noticed earlier. He plunged the rod into the ground and sent it eighteen inches down, striking nothing.

I was beginning to understand. "You think there might be another house?"

"Maybe." He pushed the rod into the ground again. "It would be odd for this rock to be here all by itself, don't you think?" He continued probing around the rock and found nothing. Then he moved a few inches to the west and pushed down on the handle. This time the rod sank only a few inches before it made a *clunk* that we all heard. Aaron said, "Fetch a shovel, Riley, and let's see what this is."

I ran for the shovel and dug out the sod, exposing a big caliche boulder. Meanwhile, Aaron kept probing the ground west of the exposed rock, and now he was getting a *clunk* almost every time he probed. We had to stop working when darkness overtook us, but by then, we had uncovered an unmistakable arc of rocks, seven of them, that looked very much like the foundation line I had exposed before.

We didn't have to beg Aaron to stay the night. He was just as anxious to finish exposing the rocks at Flint Springs as we were. He took his bedroll down to Grampy's "room" in the barn, and early the next morning we were back at the site, probing and digging. Around ten o'clock, the four of us stood arms-over-shoulders, looking down at a circle of twenty-five caliche boulders, a near-perfect copy of the foundation line that had been destroyed.

"I don't know what it is," said Aaron, "but those rocks didn't put themselves in a circle."

We even managed to locate the No Digging signs. They had been ventilated with bullet holes, and the crooks had tossed them into a ravine. With most of the bullet holes centered on the *D* in *Digging*, the signs seemed to say, No Ogging, but we figured they would get the point across and posted them around the site again.

Aaron had to go back to Sparrow to tend to some business, but he promised to clear his calendar so that he could participate in the excavation—if, of course, Dr. Montrose was still interested in coming. "And I think he will be. I'll use all my powers of persuasion on him," he said with a wink.

We weren't sure exactly what that meant, but we knew Aaron. When he made up his mind to do something, it usually got done.

He shook hands with me and Coy. "I'll try to locate Frank this afternoon. I'll call just as soon as I have some news." He turned to Mother. "Once again, dear lady, thank you for sharing your home and family with an aging bachelor."

"And once again, aging bachelor, thank you for galloping to our rescue. Your flour bombs were incredible. Will you ever cease to amaze us?"

"I hope not." He bounded into the Vega and closed the door.

I drove the truck down the road to check the "runway" for cows, and Aaron roared up into the summer sky, wagging his wings as he disappeared over the top of Hodges Mesa.

Coy walked down to the barn to play with the cats. I went into the house to do something unusual. I had decided to read some archeology on my own.

Chapter 14

Aaron called around six that evening. Coy and I raced to the phone, but he got there first. He couldn't resist sticking out his tongue at me to celebrate his little victory. I decided to take the high road and show some maturity. I didn't stick out my tongue back at him. Mother noticed and nodded her approval.

Coy talked for several minutes, then handed the phone to me.

Aaron said that he had managed to locate Dr. Montrose, who was still very interested in doing an excavation at the Flint Springs site. He had spent the week exploring a number of Plains Village ruins in the western Panhandle but had seen nothing that had the potential to be as old as our site at Flint Springs. If anything, he was more anxious to investigate than before.

"If all goes according to plan," Aaron continued, "we'll be arriving at the ranch on the first of August. Dr. Montrose hopes to bring a student from West Texas State Teacher's College to help him with the detail work and documentation. I'm hoping that you and Coy will be available to work with me as dirt donkeys."

"Dirt donkeys? That's a funny name."

"It's Frank's term for the unskilled workers, such as you and me, who labor with shovels and carry buckets of dirt to the screens. It's hard work and, this time of year, in the heat, fairly demanding. It wouldn't hurt if we could come up with another strapping man or two. Any ideas?"

"I wish we could use Spud, but he has to milk the cows twice a day and check the windmills." I thought for a moment. "We have a neighbor, Mr. Higgins. You met him when you were here in May."

"Oh yes. Nice man. Isn't he the one with the pretty daughter?"

"Uh . . . " I glanced around to see if Mr. Big Ears was listening. He was, of course, so I lowered my voice. "Why yes, now that you mention it. I suppose she is pretty."

Aaron gave a chuckle. "Does Mr. Higgins have any interest in archeology?"

"Not that I know about, but I'll work on that. I'm doing some reading on my own now. It's a lot more interesting than I ever thought."

"Excellent, Riley; I'm pleased. We're going to make a scholar out of you yet. Oh, one last item. I'll explain this to your mother in a moment, but I want you to hear it too. She's the kind of lady who goes to great lengths to make guests feel welcome and comfortable. I want it clear from the start that she'll have no responsibilities at the excavation, no cooking, cleaning, or dish washing. I've hired a man as camp cook, and we'll come prepared to sleep in tents. The crew will be entirely self-sufficient. Your mother's assignment for the next few days will be to participate as much as she wants, enjoy herself, and learn all she can about the history of your ranch."

"That's very thoughtful. I know she'll appreciate it."

"Riley, if I know your mother, she'll try to get herself right in the middle of the cooking and cleaning up if we don't watch her like a hawk. I'll depend on you to help me keep her under strict supervision. Agreed?"

"Agreed. Here, I'll let you talk to her."

Mother had been waiting for her turn. I handed her the phone and motioned for Coy to follow me outside, so that Mother could have some privacy. Out on the porch steps, Coy wanted a complete report on everything Aaron and I had discussed, so I filled him in.

He listened with interest, but then his eyes acquired a suspicious squint. "What was that business about Mr. Higgins?"

"Coy, were you eavesdropping?"

"No, I just happened to be in the same room. It's my

house too. What was it all about? And don't tell me any windy tales."

"Well, Aaron thought Mr. Higgins might want to come over and take part in the dig. I thought it was a pretty good idea."

Coy rolled his eyes. "There, you see? I ask for a straight answer, and you give me corn and malarkey. Riley, I *heard* your side of the conversation."

"Right. You were eavesdropping and invading my privacy as an American citizen."

"I did no such thing, but I know who brought up Mr. Higgins's name. You. And I know why you brought it up too."

"Because Mr. Higgins is a fine man with a strong back, and because I have reason to think he might enjoy—"

"Oh Riley, stop it! You're working on a scheme to get Laura over here. You know it and I know it."

"Laura? Coy, that's a very interesting idea. Do you suppose she might want to come?" Coy turned his eyes away from me and muttered words I couldn't hear. "No, I'm serious. It's a good idea, and I'm trying to give you credit for it."

"Riley, you never admit anything and you'd argue with a fence post, but I know what you're up to."

Just then, Mother came out onto the porch. She was smiling and didn't notice the pinched look on Coy's face. "Well, well," she said, "it sounds as though Mr. Kaplan has it all worked out and plans to make a lazybones out of me. He seems to think of everything, doesn't he?"

"Mother," said Coy, trying to deepen his squeaky voice to give it a grave tone, "Riley's working on a scheme to invite Laura Higgins to the excavation. I thought you'd want to know."

He beamed me a self-righteous little smirk.

I said, "Actually, it was . . . Laura seemed very interested when we talked about it the other day, but if you don't think it's a good idea . . . "

"I think it's a splendid idea. I'll be the only woman on the site and I would enjoy having some female companionship."

"Exactly. That's what I was just telling Coy."

Coy let out a groan. "Riley, you are the biggest—"

I pressed on. "You would have a female companion, and Mr. Higgins might be willing to help us with the heavy work. He and Laura could come together. And, well, it would give us a chance to share our interest in archeology with the neighbors."

Mother studied my face for a moment. "You thought of this yourself?"

"Oh yes, sure. As I was telling Coy, it would be *selfish* of us not to share this experience with others. I mean, it's a rare opportunity to, uh, broaden our interests and educate ourselves about the . . . the cultural resources that are right here in our own backyard."

"Cultural resources?" she said. "My, my."

I placed my hand on her shoulder and guided her back into the house, leaving Coy sitting on the step. "Mother, tomorrow I'll ride up to the flats and present the idea to Mr. Higgins, and maybe you could write a note saying that . . . well, that you approve."

"I see." Inside the house, she turned and looked me squarely in the eyes. "I'll do that, Riley, if I have your word that you'll conduct yourself as a gentleman."

"I don't know what you mean."

"You know exactly what I mean. Just give me your word, and that'll be the end of it."

"You have my word."

I figured that the lunch hour would be the best time to catch Mr. Higgins at the house. Around eleven o'clock the next morning, as I was getting ready to leave for the Higgins place, I noticed Coy sitting off by himself, folding a basketful of clothes Mother had brought in from the clothesline. Since he hadn't nagged me to take him along, I asked if he wanted to join me. He was shocked at first, then thrilled.

"You bet," he said, glancing at Mother to see if she would release him from his job.

She nodded, adding, "You boys be careful on those horses, and be back"—she glanced up at the clock—"no later than five. If you're not back by then, I'll have to send Spud to look for you. And you know how cranky he gets when we bother him at milking time."

We caught Dolly and Socks in the corral and rode

north to the head of Picket Canyon, followed a deer trail up the caprock, and climbed out onto the prairie flats. From there, it was an easy three-mile ride to the Higgins place, which occupied an area of rich farmland on the divide between the Canadian River and Wolf Creek to the north.

Coy had been quiet during the ride, but when we climbed out on top, he said, "Thanks for asking me along. Why'd you do it?"

"Are you still being suspicious?"

"Well, yes, of course I am. You play so many pranks on me, I get nervous when you turn nice all of a sudden."

I laughed. "Coy, I have no secret motives. You looked pitiful folding those clothes, and I thought you needed rescuing."

"That's all?"

"Promise."

"Well . . . thanks. It was pretty boring. Riley, if I ask you a serious question, will you give me an honest answer?" Behind his glasses, he looked even more owlish than usual.

I said, "Sure, fire away."

"Do you *like* Laura? And you know what I mean: boy-girl."

"Oh. Well . . . I don't know. But I'm beginning to think that her being a girl isn't such a terrible handicap."

Coy nodded. "I thought so. Well, that settles it."

"Settles what?"

"I'll back off."

"What are you talking about?"

He pushed his glasses up to the bridge of his nose. "I won't try to compete."

"Oh-h-h, so that's it."

"I kind of like older women, you know, but if you're interested in Laura, I'll stay out of it."

"Coy, that's very noble."

"Brothers shouldn't fight over a woman. You're the older brother and you should get the first chance."

"I really appreciate that."

"But if you stub your toe or lose interest, it'll be every man for himself."

"That's only fair. Thanks again. You're a swell guy."

Coy nodded and took a deep breath, as though a heavy burden had been lifted from his shoulders. It would have been cruel of me to laugh out loud after he had chosen the path of martyrdom, so I kept it all inside.

We reached the Higgins place around noon, just as Mr. Higgins was coming in from the field and washing up for lunch. He was glad to see us. There had been times when I hadn't felt such warmth from his wife, when I had been aware that her hawkish eyes were prowling over me, studying my clothes, fingernails, posture, and manners. But Mr. Higgins always made me feel welcome. He lived in a house with four women, and I guess that having a boy on the place was a nice change for him.

I had hoped that I might be able to conduct my business with him in private, but he invited us to come in and join them for lunch. I said no, we had eaten a big breakfast and didn't want to impose on their hospitality, so he said, "Then come and sit with us, and have a piece of hot cherry pie. Mrs. Higgins and the girls baked two this morning."

The girls were already seated at the table, three stair-stepped little angels with the same head of frizzy red hair. When Laura saw me, she blushed and looked away. When Mrs. Higgins saw me, her brows rose and she burned her finger on a pan of biscuits.

When we were all seated around the table, we bowed our heads and Mr. Higgins said grace, asking God to bless our families and thanking him for the good crops and grass, but hinting that we could use another rain.

After the family had eaten, Laura and Rachel served up the pie, made of fresh, tart cherries from Mr. Higgins's orchard behind the house. It was delicious, and I was into my second bite when Mrs. Higgins swung her gaze around to me and said, "Well! What brings you boys over here?"

I didn't dare speak with a mouth full of pie, lest I commit the felony of spurting crumbs onto the tablecloth or choking to death in front of the children, so I took my time, chewed calmly, and then launched into my presentation.

Chapter 15

I could tell that I had Mr. Higgins's attention from the start. With Mrs. Higgins, it was harder to gauge. Her interest in antiquities probably didn't run very deep, and her expression remained a bit skeptical, as though she suspected there was more to this than archeology.

When I suggested that Mr. Higgins could make a valuable contribution to the excavation team, she nodded and leaned her head forward, waiting for more, at which point I said, as casually as I could, "Oh, and Mother thought Laura might want to come too."

"Ah," said Mrs. Higgins, bobbing her head.

I gave her Mother's note. Mrs. Higgins read it with a rapid sweep of her eyes, then looked at her husband. Laura held her breath. So did I. The final verdict, it appeared, rested with her father.

Mr. Higgins made it easy. Leaning back in his

chair, he said, "You can count me in for a couple of days. I wouldn't miss it for the world. Laura?"

Laura said, "I'd love to go."

Mrs. Higgins stiffened. "Laura, honestly. Digging around in the dirt? Camping on the hard ground? That doesn't sound like something a young lady should be doing."

"Oh no," I said, "she wouldn't have to camp. She could stay at the house with Mother and sleep in a bed. Mother would enjoy the company."

All eyes went back to Mr. Higgins. "It sounds like a great adventure to me," he said. "We'll be at the site day after tomorrow, at nine o'clock sharp."

Laura beamed a smile at me.

Mr. Higgins left the table for a moment and returned with a cigar box containing a collection of artifacts he'd picked up over the years. He spread them out on the table, and that gave me the opportunity to demonstrate some of my knowledge. I explained the differences among the corner-notched Scallorn points, the side-notched Washita points, and the larger dart points. Mr. Higgins had never noticed the differences or known that they were diagnostic of different time periods. He was fascinated that most of the points in his collection weren't merely old, but ancient.

Coy and I thanked Mrs. Higgins for the pie and said our good-byes on the porch. I could see that she was still uneasy about letting Laura go to the excavation, so I made a point of giving her a firm handshake and looking directly into her eyes. "Don't worry, Mrs. Higgins. We'll take good care of Laura."

She patted my hand and managed a smile. "I know you will, Riley, but mothers worry. It's part of the job."

I didn't have a chance to speak alone with Laura, but I caught her eye as I was stepping up into the saddle. She was sparkling with excitement.

Once I had taken care of that piece of business, everything was set for the excavation, and all we had to do was wait two more days. That turned out to be the toughest part. The hours dragged by so slowly, I could hardly bear it. The following evening, the telephone rang. I had been expecting a call from Aaron.

"All's well on this end," he said. "Frank's back in town and we spent the day gathering supplies. We're ready to roll out of here at four o'clock in the morning. We should be at the site no later than nine. How about your end?"

"I've got Mr. Higgins lined up to help. Laura's coming, and Mother's fussing over her wardrobe at this very minute."

"Tell her to dress for comfort, not for style—long sleeves, loose clothing, and a wide-brimmed hat."

"You tell her. She doesn't pay any attention to me."

Aaron laughed. "On second thought, let's stay out of it. Unless something unexpected comes up, we'll meet you at Flint Springs around nine. I'm excited, and Dr.

Montrose is as giddy as a schoolboy."

We all went to bed early that night, but I couldn't sleep. After tossing and rolling in my bed for an hour, I lit a kerosene lamp and tried to read myself to sleep. I leafed through the box of literature Aaron had left and chose an article with the dreary title of "A Woodland Horizon on the Apishapa Plateau in Southeastern Colorado: The Graneros Focus," written by a Dr. Marion S. B. Woodson of the University of Colorado Department of Anthropology. Printed on brittle, yellowing paper, it looked and sounded dull enough to put me right to sleep.

Instead, it had just the opposite effect. On the second page, I encountered two paragraphs that almost leaped out at me.

> Graneros sites are characterized by small circular houses with foundations made of rock, and a tool assemblage consisting of a high percentage of corner-notched arrow points of the Scallorn type and a meager presence of thick, cord-marked pottery shards. This Plains Woodland manifestation appears to have begun around A.D. 450 and thrived until 800, when the Woodland component was replaced by a Plains Village occupation that produced side-notched arrow points and a thinner, more finely made type of pottery, similar to the ceramics found in the large Plains Village sites along the Canadian River in the western Texas Panhandle.
>
> Although these Graneros sites have not been well

documented, there is reason to think that Graneros people might have migrated southward around 800 to 900, perhaps due to a prolonged drought, and established hamlets along the Canadian River, slowly evolving their housing patterns into the mysterious Panhandle Aspect ruins recently discovered by Professor Moorehead. Unfortunately, no evidence of a Graneros occupation has ever been reported along the Canadian River.

I stared at the small print on the page, then read it again. Unless I was missing something, Dr. Woodson had just described our site at Flint Springs: small circular houses, corner-notched points, and a small amount of thick Woodland pottery. I checked the publication date at the front of the article. It had been published in 1919, eight years ago.

I blew out the lamp and stared into the darkness for what seemed an hour or more. Was it possible that Dr. Montrose had never read the Woodson article? And would I be bold enough to mention it to him? Before I could answer those questions, sleep carried me off into dreams about foundation stones, arrow points, pottery shards . . . and a young lady with frizzy red hair.

When I awoke the next morning, Mother had already prepared a big breakfast, and now she was in her room, looking for the right pair of shoes and gloves that would protect her hands without giving her the appearance of a "hay hauler."

Around 8:30, we managed to extract her from the house and got her settled in the cab of the truck. She looked splendid in her long dark dress and wide-brimmed straw hat, every hair in place, her lips and cheeks showing a hint of color, and her head held as nobly as a queen's.

I was aching to get over to the site and growled at her for being so slow. She replied, "You don't understand. All you boys have to do is jump into your jeans." We arrived at the site a little after nine, and nobody was there. Mother enjoyed a moment of vindication. "There, you see? You rush around and bully your poor mother into hurrying, and now we have to sit here and wait."

"Well, at least we're on time."

Just then, we heard the distant drone of vehicles, and off to the south we saw a cloud of dust rising above a truck loaded with equipment and Aaron's blue Chevrolet sedan pulling a water trailer. They drove up to the site and stopped.

Coy and I rushed out to greet Aaron and Dr. Montrose when they stepped out of their vehicles, and the doctor introduced us to his assistant for the dig, a college student named Lanny Douglas. He was small and wiry, almost frail in appearance, but we would soon discover that he had the energy of a jackrabbit.

The other man, Rollie Sunday, was the camp chef, a cheerful, slow-talking fellow in his fifties. He showed none of the temperament I had always associated with chuck wagon cooks, whom Grampy had often described as crabby and downright hateful. The way he told it, if you happened to wander too close to their wagon and stirred up some dust, they would scream and throw something at you—a bar of soap if a pot lid wasn't handy.

But Rollie appeared to be a man who had never known an unhappy day or ever raised his voice in anger. He taught school in Amarillo, and for him, cooking outdoors was a release from the confinement of the classroom. It appeared that Rollie would have a grand time at the dig, no matter what the rest of us did.

Mother didn't rush out to greet the men but came behind us at her own pace, floating along with an open umbrella resting on her shoulder. The sight of her caused Aaron and Dr. Montrose to stop talking and stare.

Dr. Montrose walked over to the hole left by Vernon McElroy and his friends. He looked down at it and shook his head. "This past week, I've seen this repeated dozens of times: houses plundered, pristine village sites that have laid undisturbed for a thousand years torn apart and destroyed. Aaron, I'll wager that more archeology has been obliterated along this river in the past ten years than has been excavated in the entire United States since Jamestown. It saddens me." He turned to me. "But you and your brother got it stopped, young Riley, and for that I'm grateful."

"Aaron did. Mostly I just watched. Did he tell you what happened?"

"He said you called the sheriff." When I told him the

story about Aaron dropping flour bombs on the crooks, he could hardly believe it and stared at Aaron with a mixture of shock and admiration. Aaron seemed a little embarrassed hearing his exploits recounted. He fidgeted and occasionally shrugged one shoulder. The doctor threw back his head and roared with laughter. "Well done, Aaron; by golly, well done! That warms my soul."

Coy and I helped unload the equipment and set up three army tents that had survived the Great War in Europe. They had come from Aaron's legendary warehouse, where they had sat for several years after he'd bought them at an auction of surplus military equipment. Inside one of the tents, we assembled a camp stove made of steel plate, and ran a stovepipe through a hole in the roof. Rollie Sunday gathered an armload of mesquite wood and soon had a big pot of coffee bubbling on the stove.

By ten o'clock, Laura and her father still hadn't arrived, and I began to fear that Mrs. Higgins had changed the plans. But then we saw the Higgins's Dodge coming down the hill from the east.

Mr. Higgins's face was tight when he stepped out of the car. "Sorry we're late, Riley." He gestured toward Laura. "I had her up this morning before daylight to give her time to get ready. Next time, I'll keep her up all night."

I laughed and told Mr. Higgins that I understood.

Laura climbed out just then, looking as cool and serene as a dish of lime sherbet, wearing a light green dress and a white straw hat with a ribbon tied under her chin. She smiled at me and waved the tips of her fingers in greeting. "Hello, Riley. Are we terribly late?"

I stared at her. "Oh, I don't think you mitched muss."

Coy was beside me, gaping like a monkey. "Holy smokes, is *that* Laura Higgins?"

"Put your eyeballs back in your head," I whispered. "It's not polite to stare."

But he continued to stare, and so did I.

While we finished setting up the camp, Dr. Montrose and Lanny Douglas worked with a surveyor's transit, laying out "grid lines" for the excavation. The transit was a kind of telescope mounted on a tripod, and they used it to establish the elevations and precise measurements for the excavation unit. This was our first glimpse at the strict discipline and precision the doctor would impose on the project, the first hint that every square inch of dirt that fell within his grid had now become part of a controlled scientific experiment.

Squinting into the transit and calling out numbers, Francis Montrose ceased being the affable gentleman we had known before and became a gruff, tight-lipped, serious man of science.

It was slow, tedious work. Dr. Montrose and Lanny laid out their grid with measuring tapes marked with metric units instead of conventional feet and inches. After measuring, remeasuring, and mapping the entire site, they laid out a working unit two meters square that covered the interior of the circular house and some ground that lay outside the rock outline. They marked the boundaries of the unit with string tied to long nails driven into the ground.

This unit would be the focus of the excavation, the point at which surgeon Montrose would apply his scalpel and conduct the operation.

Chapter 16

At noon, we stopped for a light lunch of apples, pears, cheese, and sausage, then continued the work. Around three o'clock, Dr. Montrose finished laying out the site and called us together for instructions.

"Ladies and gentlemen, we're about ready to start the excavation. What we have here"—he gestured toward the circle of rocks—"is something I've never seen before. Frankly, I don't know what it is, whether it's a house, a storage pit, or something else. We don't have the time or the manpower to expose the entire structure—it would take a week or more, and I have to get back to Boston before then. So we'll do a test unit, two meters square, across the center.

"Our primary research objective will be to find the floor. A floor is important because it gives us context:

whatever material we find on the floor is what they were using at the time they abandoned the structure. Any artifacts we find above floor level are out of context, probably trash deposited by later occupants of this ridge. That material will be more recent and out of context with the structure."

Mr. Higgins asked, "Sir, how do we know if it was a house or something else?"

Dr. Montrose nodded. "Most prehistoric houses in the Southern Plains had a central hearth, where the occupants did their cooking and warmed themselves. If this was a house, we should encounter the remnants of a hearth, as well as some evidence of what they were eating—very important information. Bone will tell us if they were eating bison or smaller animals. To find seeds that are too small to show up in our screens, we'll bag soil samples off the floor, take them back to the lab, and pour them into a basin of water. The seeds and organic material will float, and we'll examine them under a microscope."

Mother asked, "What kind of seeds are we talking about?"

"Woodland people were hunter-gatherers, so I would be very surprised to find any charred corn fragments. That came in later occupations with farming. I would expect to find various kinds of wild grasses, wild plum, hackberry, goosefoot, and possibly wild sunflower seeds."

Mother thought for a moment. "I don't want to sound

dumb, but how could seeds survive in the ground for a thousand years or more? Wouldn't they decompose?"

I was glad she had asked. I had wondered about that myself.

Dr. Montrose gave her a smile. "Excellent question, Mrs. McDaniels, and you're exactly right. Organic material decomposes unless it has been burned. Carbon doesn't decompose, so whatever specimens we find will have been charred in the fire."

His face grew solemn and he ran his gaze over the group. "I'm glad you're all here. I want you to enjoy yourselves, but you mustn't forget that you're part of a controlled excavation. Everything we do inside that unit must be documented. Every ounce of dirt must be screened, every artifact mapped in, and every bit of cultural material bagged according to depth. If I bark at you now and then, please don't be offended. I understand that you're volunteers, but we must try to maintain strict controls in our work. If I publish our results in a scientific journal, it will be scrutinized by a small audience of very critical readers. They can be extremely cruel when they find evidence of shoddy research, and it will be the hide on my back that feels the lash." He arched his brows and smiled. "Okay folks, let's get started."

Our first task was to clear the two-meter unit of the "overburden," the soil that had covered the site over the centuries, through the effects of wind and water erosion. We removed it with flat shovels. Dr. Montrose showed us how to "shovel-skim" the overburden, slipping the blade of the shovel beneath the soil and pushing so that the path of the shovel left a surface that was flat and level.

He told us to do the shovel work in pairs. Since I was anxious to get to started, I took one of the shovels, and Aaron took the other. We skimmed off the soil and threw it into a pile outside the working unit. It seemed easy at first, but within half an hour, I found myself leaning on my shovel handle, panting for breath and dripping sweat.

When Mr. Higgins offered to take my shovel, I was glad to give it up. I had thought I was in pretty good physical shape, but this was hard work. I felt a bit better, though, when after twenty minutes, Mr. Higgins's tongue was hanging out, at which time Coy took a turn. He wore out in a hurry, and I was ready to go back to work. Aaron worked at a steady pace and didn't ask for any relief.

When we had removed eighteen inches of overburden from the unit, Dr. Montrose noticed something and told the diggers to stop. He stepped down into the unit and studied the soil.

"This," he said, pointing to some dark spots, "is what we're looking for. These are flecks of ash and charcoal, and they tell us that we're through the overburden and have come to the occupation level. You see how the soil has turned darker?"

I peered down at the surface of the unit. Once he had pointed out the dark stain in the soil, I could see it, but if he hadn't pointed it out, I wouldn't have noticed. That little shadow of soil was very subtle, and it required a sharp, trained eye to spot it.

Dr. Montrose continued. "This soil change is very important. Notice how the dirt has a kind of greasy appearance. This is a cultural zone where the occupants were building fires and cooking meat. Now we slow down and put the shovels away."

Lanny and Dr. Montrose stepped inside the unit and checked the depth with a string level and measuring tape. They skimmed off a few high spots with shovels, until they had the unit as level and square as a box made of wood, and at that point they were ready to begin working with trowels and brushes.

I had hoped I might be chosen for a troweling job, but Dr. Montrose had already decided to use Mother and Laura instead. When he saw the disappointment on my face, he said, "I've found that women have more patience for detail work than boys. Besides, we need dirt donkeys to carry buckets to the screen."

He demonstrated proper troweling technique to Mother and Laura, shaving the top layer of soil with long, even strokes, then sweeping up the loose dirt with a brush and placing it into one of the buckets. Mother and Laura exchanged uneasy glances, sensing that they had overdressed for the occasion, but they gathered up their skirts, got down on their knees, and began troweling.

When they had filled the first bucket, Lanny Douglas carried it over to the shaker screen and demonstrated screening technique. He dumped the bucket of dirt into a screen and gave it a vigorous shake, causing the smaller particles of dirt to pass through the quarter-inch mesh wire. Then, propping the screen on one knee, he ran his hand over the material that remained.

"What you're looking for is any material that is cultural, anything that bears the mark of a human." He rubbed his hand over the contents of the screen and began pulling out examples of cultural material for us to study. "Here's a fragment of bone, probably deer. This is a cracked boiling stone. You can see that it's been burned in a fire. Save it. This is burned bone. These are flint flakes, definitely cultural. Ah, and this"—he held up a small piece of something white—"is a fragment of freshwater mussel shell. Already we've learned something about their diet. They were harvesting mussels from the spring and bringing them back here. They cracked them open, ate the meat, and used the shells as spoons and digging tools."

He took one last look at the pebbles in the screen and gave it an upward jerk, clearing the screen. "The rest we don't need." He opened his hand and showed us the material he had saved, then dropped it into a paper specimen bag. "That is typical of what you're likely to find, but now and then, the screener will get lucky and find an artifact the trowelers have missed: a scraper, an arrow point, a shard of pottery, even a bead made of bone or clay. If you find something in the screen that you don't recognize or understand, call me or Dr. Montrose."

Aaron and Mr. Higgins operated the two screens, while Coy and I lugged buckets of dirt to the screeners, hefted them up to the level of the screens, and dumped them.

Once we all understood our jobs, the work began to take on the appearance of a well-oiled machine, while Dr. Montrose floated from one location to another, keeping a sharp eye out for anything unusual and making notes on a clipboard. Lanny stepped into the unit and began troweling next to Mother.

Around seven o'clock we began catching whiffs of something good coming from Rollie Sunday's cooking fire, and at seven thirty he rang a bell, calling us to supper. While we stacked our shovels and gathered up tools, Dr. Montrose looked through the specimen bags and made notes.

Rollie had made a table out of planks and barrels, and we formed a line and filled our tin plates with barbecued pork ribs, potato salad, carrot strips, and canned peaches. We had all worked up a big appetite and didn't leave much in the serving pans. I drifted over to Laura and sat down beside her to eat. I asked how she had enjoyed her first day as an archeologist.

"It's fun and very interesting," she said, "but I'm surprised how tired I am. I'm not used to being out in the hot sun. Aren't you exhausted?"

"Me? No. It wasn't bad at all." I didn't want to tell her

that I was worn to a frazzle and was ready to crawl into my bedroll.

After supper, Rollie washed dishes in a big tub, while Dr. Montrose and Lanny retired to their tent to write up their daily field notes. The rest of us sat around the fire. Mr. Higgins brought out a harmonica and played some sad old Civil War songs. Then Aaron got his violin out of the car, and they played together while the fire died to glowing red embers.

I found myself staring at Laura's face in profile until she turned suddenly and caught me gawking. Then I made a determined effort to look at something else.

Mother wanted to drive back to the house before darkness fell, so she and Laura left in the truck around eight thirty. Dr. Montrose, Aaron, and Lanny slept in one of the tents, while Coy, Mr. Higgins, and I rolled out our beds in the other. Rollie Sunday set up a cot in the cook tent and slept with the groceries and Dutch ovens. He snored all night long.

Rollie was up before daylight, building his fire and getting the breakfast started. Soon the smells of fresh coffee and frying bacon drifted over the camp, and the men emerged from their tents and lined up in front of the big coffeepot. I crept out of the tent, leaving Coy to catch a few more winks of sleep, and noticed that every muscle in my body ached. I hobbled around and took my place in the coffee line with the men. When my turn came, Rollie filled my tin cup with hot black liquid.

I had never cared much for coffee, but this seemed

the time to give it another try—drinking campfire coffee at sunrise with a group of men. Rollie watched as I took my first sip. "How's the java?"

"Great," I lied. I wanted to gag. It tasted awful! I carried the cup around for a while, just to keep up appearances, then pitched it onto the screen pile when nobody was looking.

Dr. Montrose was anxious to get started, so we had to gulp down our eggs and bacon, and by the time the sun slipped over the top of the caprock, we were back at work. Mother and Laura drove into camp thirty minutes later and seemed to be having a great time talking about flowers and clothes, pie-making, gardening, and recipes—subjects Mother had little opportunity to discuss with Grampy and us boys. I noticed that they had both chosen to wear more practical clothing: simple cotton dresses, and sunbonnets instead of hats.

The first few hours brought very little in the way of excitement. The trowelers troweled, the screeners screened, and we dirt donkeys kept the heavy buckets of dirt moving to the screens. Then, around ten o'clock, Mother's trowel made a pinging sound that brought Dr. Montrose over at a trot.

He squinted down into the unit and talked in a low voice with Lanny Douglas. Then he turned to Mother with sparkling eyes and said, "I think you've found the central hearth, Mrs. McDaniels. It's clay-lined and appears to be a very nice one. This is a house, no question about it."

Chapter 17

The discovery of the hearth was an indication that the trowelers had reached the floor level, and at that point the work became a lot more interesting. Lanny exposed a piece of yellowed bone, which Dr. Montrose identified as the scapula of a deer, used as a tool for digging. Mr. Higgins found a hide scraper and a fragment of a bone awl in his screen, and Aaron came up with a perfect little Scallorn point.

Laura scraped away with her trowel and found nothing—until noon, when she unearthed twelve large shards of thick Woodland pottery lying on the floor level. Dr. Montrose was very excited. After making a drawing of the shards on a piece of paper, he removed them one by one and began fitting them together.

"I think they come from one pot, and when we get

them glued together, we'll have the entire upper half, including the rim. This is outstanding."

By the end of the day, we were all sunburned, wind-blown, and tired to the bone, but we had managed to finish the unit and had met Dr. Montrose's research objectives. Suddenly, it was all over. The next day, we would backfill the unit to restore the site to its original condition, break down the camp, and go back to the normal world.

Coy and I were standing beside the unit, looking into it, when Lanny Douglas joined us. "That doesn't look like much for two days of hard work, does it?"

Lanny had read my mind. "It sure doesn't. For all my blisters and sore muscles, there ought to be a hole ten feet deep and a hundred feet across."

Lanny chuckled. "Just be glad we didn't dig the whole house."

Coy groaned. "I can't imagine!"

"But," said Lanny, "Dr. Montrose did it right. Everything was documented. The next question is, what does it all mean?"

I looked into his face. "What *does* it all mean?"

"I don't know, but the boss seems pretty excited."

After supper, we sat around the fire and listened as Dr. Montrose gave us a summary of the work we had done.

"Folks, what we've uncovered here is a circular stone structure with a central hearth and an east-facing entryway, and the artifacts lying on the floor are unmistakably from the Woodland period. The house could have been occupied as much as fifteen hundred years ago, and"—he beamed—"it's unprecedented. No one has ever exposed or documented a Woodland structure in the Texas Panhandle, and no one ever dreamed that, once we found one, it would turn out to be circular. Woodland structures in Missouri, Nebraska, and eastern Oklahoma are square or rectangular. Where this circular architecture came from, I can't imagine."

I was staring into the fire, listening to the thumping of my heart and wondering if I would be brave enough to speak. Before I had time to think, I heard myself say, "Had you thought about the Graneros focus?"

Dead silence fell over the group, and every eye swung around to me. Dr. Montrose said, "What did you say?"

Suddenly I felt very awkward and regretted that I had opened my mouth. What did I know about anything? But it was too late to back out now, so I swallowed my fear and plunged on. "The Graneros people built circular houses of stone, and they were from the Woodland period."

"Yes, but they were up in Colorado, and there has never been . . . " Dr. Montrose and Lanny traded glances. "Where did you hear about Graneros?"

"In one of the articles you left. It was so old, the paper was falling apart. The author thought the Graneros people might have migrated down into the Canadian River valley."

The doctor stepped toward me. "Go on. Can you remember the source?"

"It was written by a Professor Woodson from the University of Colorado."

"And the date? Do you remember when it was published?"

"1919, I think."

Dr. Montrose ran his hand through his hair and gazed up at the sky. "Of course. I read that piece years ago and had forgotten about it. Woodson's theory was considered outrageous at the time, and no one paid much attention to it. Riley, this is good. I'll want to see that article."

The group broke into applause and I was given slaps on the back by everyone present, even my little brother. Mother stared at me in amazement, as though she couldn't believe that her elder son had done something other than cause mischief.

I turned and met Laura's blue eyes. A little smile played across her mouth and she raised one eyebrow, as if to say, "Well, look at you!"

That sent a tingle down my spine. I turned my eyes back to the front and tried to listen to Dr. Montrose, but my mind had strayed from bone fragments and soil texture.

The next morning we rose at first light and feasted on another of Rollie Sunday's camp breakfasts: scrambled eggs and sausage, rolled up in tortillas, and fried potatoes and onions. I made another attempt to drink his cowboy coffee and came to the same conclusion I'd reached the day before: a cup of hot tar couldn't have been worse. I pitched it out when nobody was looking.

To my annoyance, Coy poured himself a cup and drank it down to the dregs—and did it in a very conspicuous manner, so that everyone noticed. Drifting past me, he said, "There's nothing like coffee cooked over a mesquite fire, is there?"

In a low voice, I said, "Are you actually drinking that stuff?"

"Sure. Aren't you?"

"Of course. It's swell."

Mother and Laura arrived late, and ate the portions of food Rollie had saved for them. Dr. Montrose had asked Mother to bring the Woodson article from the house, and she had remembered. She gave it to him, and he and Lanny Douglas sat on overturned dirt buckets and discussed the passages on Graneros architecture. I couldn't hear what they were saying, but their heads were nodding, and when Dr. Montrose looked up and caught my eye, he gave me a smile and the "okay" sign.

After breakfast, we plunged into the task of breaking down camp and packing all the equipment onto the truck. Coy helped Rollie Sunday "bust the suds," his term for washing up all the breakfast dishes in his big washtub, while Aaron, Mr. Higgins, and I collapsed the tents and rolled them up with their poles and stakes. Mother and Laura helped Lanny Douglas catalog the artifacts in the specimen bags, while Dr. Montrose prowled over the site, making a few final notes on his clipboard.

After we had packed and loaded the tents, Aaron, Mr. Higgins, and I plunged into the task of backfilling the unit—shoveling the screened dirt into buckets and dumping it back into the hole. I was surprised that Dr. Montrose would cover up a hole we had spent so much time creating, but he explained that he had gotten the information he needed and wanted to leave the land as close to its undisturbed state as possible.

By ten o'clock we had everything packed and loaded, leaving no sign of our presence except a few spots of bare dirt and trampled grass. Dr. Montrose worked his way through the group, shaking hands and thanking us for our hard work and excellent effort. When he came to me, he gripped my hand and gave me a warm smile.

"Riley, you've made a special contribution, and I can't thank you enough. On the train back east, I'll do some woodshedding on the Graneros article. You may have given me the ideas I need for writing up our results."

Mother was standing nearby, and I could see that she was proud.

We said our good-byes, and Dr. Montrose, Lanny, and Rollie climbed into the truck and began the long drive back to Amarillo, where Dr. Montrose would catch his train. Aaron lingered awhile longer, as though he hated to leave, but he promised Mother that he would come again.

"Would you consider coming for Thanksgiving?" she asked.

"I'll let you know." He shook hands with me and Coy. "Once again, it's been a pleasure sharing your company. You're both fine boys, and I know your mother is very proud of you."

He hurried to his car and drove away.

Mr. Higgins and Laura were the last to leave. Mr. Higgins had enjoyed himself enormously and said he couldn't remember when he'd spent two more pleasant days. While he was thanking Mother for including him in the excavation, I found myself standing beside Laura and wondering what to say.

"I'm glad you came," I finally managed.

She gave me a quick smile and looked away. "Having a girl around wasn't too much of a burden?"

"Not at all. You, uh, did some good work, finding that pottery, and . . . Laura, I'm really glad you came."

"Will you come see me before school starts?"

"Yes, even if I have to crawl."

"Oh, don't crawl. You'd get stickers." Her gaze drifted to her father, who was still talking to Mother, and before I knew it, her hand found mine and gave it a squeeze. "Bye."

Just for an instant, we were holding hands! Blood rushed to my face, and an electrical sensation moved across my scalp.

Then, just as suddenly, it was over, leaving me wondering if it had actually happened. Laura went to her father and laid her head on his shoulder until he had finished talking, then they walked, arm in arm, to their car. She opened her door and paused for one last wave goodbye, her long red hair floating in the wind.

As they drove away, I heard Mother sigh. "Well, that was an experience to remember. What a nice group of people." I realized that she was watching me, her head cocked to the side and a lopsided smile on her mouth. "Riley, you look different somehow. Older."

"It's probably the suntan. Let's go home. I'll drive."

I slipped my arm through hers, walked her to the truck, opened the door for her, and helped her up into the seat. As I was walking around to the other side, Coy fell in step beside me. His eyes had taken on a suspicious squint. "Riley, what was going on between you and Laura?"

"I don't know what you're talking about."

"Oh please! Am I blind and stupid? I saw your face, and you were whispering about something."

"Oh, that. We were discussing those twelve shards of pottery Laura found. We agreed that it was a very interesting discovery and that we'd like to do some more reading on archeology."

His stared at me for a moment, then his eyelids sank. "Riley, you are the biggest . . . "

We climbed into the cab of the truck and headed for home.

Chapter 18

The Wednesday before Thanksgiving was a cold, sunny afternoon. Mother, Coy, and I were bundled up in winter coats and hats, standing in front of the house and looking off into the distance.

All the trees on the ranch had changed into the autumn colors of yellow, gold, and brown, and the tall grass on the edges of the canyons had added splashes of red. The wind had fallen to a whisper, and in the distance we heard a faint hum.

Coy, who always wanted to be the first to notice everything, said, "There it is. That's Aaron."

We shaded our eyes and looked toward the sound. Sure enough, a speck of blue appeared above Hodges Mesa, and Aaron's Vega banked left and headed toward our house. He had called the day before on our private phone and asked if he was still invited for Thanksgiving. Naturally, we were delighted. And then he added a bit of mystery. "I have something special to show you."

We weren't surprised that he would be bringing something. He always did. We were all anxious to see what it would be this time.

He stepped out of the plane, looking fresh and dapper in a three-piece wool suit and a tie, and a pair of black cowboy boots polished to a shine. I noticed that he was carrying something in his left hand, a book or a magazine. After we had said our greetings, his dark eyes roamed the canyons, and he sighed. "It's little wonder that people have lived here for thousands of years. Who would ever want to leave such a place?" His gaze drifted down and settled on me. He handed me the object he was carrying. "This is for you, young sir."

It appeared to be a scholarly journal, and it bore the weighty title *Bulletin of the Southwestern Archeological Society*, Volume XII.

"Oh. Thank you," I managed to say. "More reading on archeology?" To be honest, if this was his surprise, I was a little disappointed. I had expected something more spectacular: a live tiger or a falcon perched on his shoulder. Despite all of our excitement over the summer, I wasn't exactly thrilled at the prospect of reading another article on archeology.

"There's one article that I think you'll find particularly interesting." He took the journal and flipped to the front. "Here. 'Evidence of a Graneros Structure in the Texas Panhandle.'"

"Dr. Montrose wrote up the results of our excavation?"

Aaron nodded. "He did indeed, and I believe he set a new speed record for getting an article into print. These things sometimes take years. Turn to page thirty-seven." I turned to the page and saw the title at the top. Aaron said, "Look closer. Do you see anything unusual?" I didn't. "Riley, look at the list of authors."

I looked . . . and almost fainted with surprise. "Mother, look! It says, 'Francis Montrose, Ph.D., Lanny Douglas, B.S., and Riley McDaniels.' He listed me as one of the authors!"

Mother grabbed the journal and stared at the page, as though she couldn't believe it. She gave me a hug and almost cried. "Lawsy me, child, six months ago I wasn't even sure you could read!"

Later, as we sat down at the table, Aaron lifted his glass of apple cider. "I propose a toast to Riley McDaniels: protector of antiquities and famous author."

We clinked our glasses together and ate the best Thanksgiving dinner I could ever remember.

Author's Note

The information presented here on archeology in the Texas Panhandle is based on twelve years of research I have done as an amateur archeologist—an amateur who has worked in association with professionals in the field and who has tried to protect the prehistoric sites on his own land. Although I have taken a few liberties in transposing current thinking on archeology into the time frame of the 1920s, the details about artifacts, the stages of prehistoric development, and the methods used by professional archeologists are correct and based on first-hand experience, as well as considerable reading on the subject.

The theory of a migration of the Woodland Graneros people from southeastern Colorado into the Texas Panhandle was proposed by Dr. Robert G. Campbell in a book called *The Panhandle Aspect of the Chaquaqua Plateau* (Texas Tech Graduate Studies, 1976). No evidence of such a migration has yet been documented, and as of this writing no one has ever found a Woodland house in the Texas Panhandle. This continues to baffle those of us who wonder how sophisticated multiroom houses made of stone could have appeared along the Canadian River around A.D. 1250 when there was no record of house building in the Woodland period that preceded it.

Archeologists have advanced several theories to explain it, involving the physical migration of people, the transmission of ideas from one group to another, and an indigenous development of stone architecture. I find Dr. Campbell's theory as plausible as any of the others, and maybe even more plausible. The problem is that no one has been able to prove the case one way or the other through excavation and carbon dating. Hence, we might say that the events described in this book are the day-dreams of an amateur archeologist who would like to find answers to some nagging questions.

In April of 2002, an excavation team led by Brett Cruse of the Texas Historical Commission spent five days testing two circular stone structures on my ranch in Roberts County, Texas. These odd circles of rock occurred on a ridge toe where surface artifacts and debris suggested a longtime Woodland occupation, with very little evidence of a later Plains Village component. When we began the excavation, we had reason to suspect that the stone foundations would turn out to be Woodland structures, and that they might actually give us proof of the kind of

Graneros presence in the Panhandle that Dr. Campbell had proposed in his 1976 study.

But carbon dates from ash in the central hearth in one of the structures gave a date range of A.D. 1450–1600. These were not Graneros structures, but rather ephemeral houses built by protohistorical nomads who camped there for a short time while following bison herds across the plains. This wasn't the information we had hoped to find, but serious archeology is devoted to finding what is actually there, not what we wish might be there. As Dr. Montrose might say, "Evidence first, then conclusions." Graneros structures in the Panhandle, if they exist at all, are still waiting for a team of energetic archeologists to find them.

I hope that I have managed to pass along to the reader some of my enthusiasm for archeology. I would be especially pleased if readers carried away a sense of urgency about the importance of protecting prehistoric sites from amateur plundering. Whether well-intentioned or not, digging into ancient ruins destroys the context of a site, erasing our memory of the people who occupied this land long ago, and who were part of the human adventure upon this blue planet of ours. That is something worth protecting.